All-American Coke Whore

M. J. Scott

I give my love to my family and friends.

1

It always takes the coldest night in January for a car's heater to stop working. The check engine light had been on since Tuesday, and the Chevy Cobalt rumbled and shook whenever Faith took it over 70 on the highway. She convinced herself that she'd probably die in her car one day, and scowled knowing she'd have to take it to a shop and pay out the ass for whatever needed to be done. It was just one more thing to go on top of the shitty apartment, shitty clothes, and shitty condition that she was in. A car on the verge of another breakdown would be the cherry on top of her shitty life a la mode.

Faith shivered and watched her breath turn to vapor. It left a morose expression on her face, already covered in heavy mascara and cheap cosmetics. She felt anger and sadness twisting inside her stomach. This is where all those aspirations of a young girl had led her; all that hope and perceived confidence, all those dreams of meeting the right boy who would take her far away.

Every choice she'd ever made had brought her to this point. Driving across town in a busted Cobalt, all so she could meet a stranger to fuck for cold hard cash. She felt her eyes begin to moisten and had to force her composure before making the next left turn into the hotel parking lot. Faith dried her eyes on her shirt and re-examined her face in the rear-view mirror, annoyed that she'd now have to re-apply her mascara. She'd been in the business long enough to know that she would have to put her feelings aside for the next hour and become the actress she always wanted to be. The night's salary was on the line and she couldn't risk not making her $200; especially with business being slow since December.

Faith had created a strict code to live by when she started prostituting herself. If the client played nice and treated her well, she'd want to give him a good fuck that would make him call her again the next time he was in the market for snatch. If he was a jerk, well, then it didn't matter as much but she still didn't want him thinking she was a basket case. If he did, then there was always the risk that he'd change his mind and close the door before she had a chance to pocket the money.

Faith touched up her makeup then reached into her purse, pulling out a small Ziploc containing mid-grade cocaine, along with a tube of water-based lube that she sat on her lap while preparing the rest of her routine. She was going to need both additives in order to blow and fuck the man she was about to meet for the first time. Sticking her hand in the bag, she gathered some of the powder with her finger nail and brought it up to her nose, ingesting it all with one snort. She had to sniffle hard three times to get it past the winter mucus buildup. The drug burned the inside of her nostrils, but soon enough she was able to taste the familiar bitterness that trailed from the nasal tract down to her throat. To make this into a full-course meal, she reached behind her seat for the Smirnoff that was lying on the back floorboard, unscrewed the cap, and took a healthy swig from the bottle.

She had to cut down her intake lately with money being so tight. Fortunately for her, that glorious hit would likely be enough to last her until the end of her appointment. If she was lucky, the asshole would have his own party favors and let her ride on that during her stay. Smiling at the rush of euphoria hitting her body, Faith picked up the lubricant and squirted a pinch of gel onto her index finger before rubbing it along the inner walls of her vagina. Now ready to meet her client she stepped out of the car and felt the windchill press against her back. Faith shivered with the sudden cold, wishing that she were still at home in her pajamas, drinking a hot beverage, and watching TV.

"This better be worth it, I swear to God," she said aloud, slamming the car door and making her way to the hotel.

Faith saw the gentleman standing by the emergency exit and wondered if he'd been there since they talked on the phone. She sized him up from a distance and assumed he was nice enough; probably traveling for work and wanting to get some play. Or, maybe he had one too many hang ups with his wife or girlfriend and needed to comfort himself with paid sex. Whichever the case, judging by his demeanor Faith believed he would be an easy job regardless.

The man waved to Faith and she politely waved back. He wasn't particularly attractive, but they never really were. Attractive men with money didn't have to pay for her kind of company, and if they did, they were going to shop for a high-class escort with fake tits and the body of a porn star. Faith would have loved a spot in that category, but she understood how the world worked and knew she'd have to make do with being another coke-fueled hooker on call.

Her light blue eyes, olive skin, and tattoos made her look exotic and gave men the impression that she would be into some kinks if the case permitted. She also had a pretty face, round ass, and a nice pair of tits on her chest. However, the extra weight around her belly, cleft lip scar, and elongated labia minora would keep her from getting a star on the boulevard.

The client had on blue jeans with a red sweatshirt, and sported hair that looked like it had just been in the shower. Faith picked up from past experiences that what a man wore when meeting her communicated a great deal about who he was and how he would treat her.

If he greeted her in sweatpants and a grease-stained t-shirt, it usually meant that he was lonely and if Faith showed the slightest hint of affection, he'd likely pay an extra $200 for a second hour of her time. Unfortunately, this also meant that he wasn't regularly hygienic and she'd have to deal with the vinegary scent of his balls when she went down on him. This category of men sadly made up a growing number of her clients - pathetic, smelly, losers. But at least they had plenty of money to give her since they obviously weren't spending it on a girlfriend.

She tried to be moderately friendly toward these types, knowing they were already self-conscious enough. Starting with a blowjob to get them ready, she would listen to their quivers and wait for them to get hard enough so she could move on to the next act. Once they were erect, she'd maneuver herself onto them, placing her pussy directly in front of their faces so they could awkwardly eat her out while she sucked on their small cocks. She got no pleasure out of letting them stick their tongues inside her. Faith only did it because it gave her a break from having to look at their faces.

It was always better to be on top for these customers, or opt for doggy style if they were determined to be in charge. The missionary position was a dangerous game so she tried to stay away from it. The weight of their fat would press down on her, making it feel as though she were on the brink of suffocation. She'd have to take shallow breaths and wait for their inevitable grunt to signal when they blew their load. The whole process, regardless of the position, would take approximately four minutes.

On the flip side of the coin, if the man dressed nicely - typically in slacks, a button-up, and an overpriced haircut, it usually meant that he had an inflated sense of self-worth and was going to be the most demanding. Or, he'd want to do some bizarre shit that she'd need another bump of coke to get through. These were the men who typically had drugs and liquor in their rooms so Faith was happy to let them play the gentleman; wining and dining her before they got down to business.

The most vanilla of the group were the ones who ordered her around, and then became whiny pricks when they weren't getting the service they hoped for. Faith had a severe loathing for this type of customer and would often try to end their dates long before their hour was up.

The second category in this lot were the men who saw her tattoos and believed that she would be the one to satisfy their perversions. Many of them were fans of sticking their tongues up her ass; but for some, they would pay a high price to fulfill the fetishes they could only discuss with a woman like her.

Over her tenure as an escort, Faith had become jaded to anal play, milking the prostate, pretending to be a relative, and mild BDSM.

7

The strangest thing to occur, however, was when she visited a hot shot lawyer's condo and found herself defecating on a glass coffee table while he laid underneath stroking his dick. The situation was already unnatural for her, but the kicker was when he stopped her on the way to bathroom to clean herself off.

It took some negotiation and an extra $500 before Faith was willing to accept him railing her from behind in the state she was in. Needing the money and urgently wanting to get the night over with, she bent over the couch with her ass in the air while he enthusiastically fucked her. The lawyer groaned in ecstasy while her fecal matter smeared on his stomach like a Rorschach painting. Faith closed her eyes and hoped he'd finish soon, all while feeling rationally nervous that she'd wind up with a nasty UTI.

In her earlier days as an escort, Faith would have told him to go fuck off after making that kind of proposition. Over time though the line blurred between the things she would and wouldn't do for money. As her self-respect waned, as did her dignity.

So, being that this guy looked normal and was wearing the standard jeans and sweatshirt combo, Faith presumed that he was probably clean, showered, and likely wouldn't ask her to do anything too out of the ordinary.

2

It was showtime.

Wanting to escape the 34-degrees outside Faith picked up the pace and put forth her best attempt at a smile.

"Andrew?" she asked, making sure he was the guy who called her.

"Yeah," he replied, nervously checking the parking lot for anyone who could be watching them. "Let's go in through the side door. I don't want the front desk to see us."

Faith thought it was sweet of him, but also dumb. Wanting to avoid the front desk at a hotel was the sign of someone meeting an escort for the first time in their life. Regular hobbyists knew that as long as they kept their cool and remained inconspicuous, neither the desk clerk or the cleaning crew were going to give a rat's ass.

Faith followed Andrew through the side door and to the elevator. He suggested taking the stairs to avoid passing strangers, but Faith refused since she was wearing heels and wasn't about to hurt her feet climbing a staircase for this man.

Andrew scanned his keycard at the door and waited for the red light to turn green. As soon as Faith followed him in, she instinctively began looking around for anything that could signify a police sting, or a clue that Andrew was a dangerous client. Women in her profession learn how to quickly gauge a hotel room for irregularities. It becomes an important survival tactic for those who don't want to find themselves locked up or dead in a dumpster.

Andrew hadn't shown any signs that he was up to anything suspicious. If anything, he was the jumpy one; still worried that

Faith was going to say a code word and have police bust through the door to put him in cuffs.

There was an expensive camera sitting on the dresser that caught Faith's attention. She brushed it off, assuming that Andrew was probably either a professional photographer, or he wanted to make a sex tape which she would charge him extra for.

The only other quirks were the empty suitcases in the corner and the stash of groceries sitting on the dresser. No one unpacks like this at a hotel and then makes a grocery trip unless they're staying for a while. Faith wondered if he was living in the hotel, but didn't bother asking because she didn't care enough to find out. This was just a job and she was already sick of being there. All she wanted was to make it through the next hour so she could go home, change into something more comfortable, and drink herself to sleep.

"I've never actually done this kind of thing before," Andrew said, standing uneasily near the bed while Faith removed her coat.

Faith had difficulty showing empathy, but tried to muster some regardless. "That's okay, sweetie. Just give me the money and I'll take care of the rest."

"Oh yeah, of course," Andrew agreed, reaching for his wallet and pulling out ten fresh twenty-dollar bills. He handed over the cash and watched Faith stuff it in her purse. With the monetary exchange complete Faith looked at the nearest bed and Andrew took this as his cue to make himself comfortable.

"Just relax," Faith said, pleased now that she had her money and was standing in a warm room.

The cocaine and vodka were kicking in so she felt loose enough mentally, and the lube sloshing inside her was surely going to help as well. She cracked a half smile to Andrew while taking off her shirt and bra. She then slid her skirt and v-string down to her ankles. Now fully nude, Faith gave Andrew a few moments to stare at her pierced nipples and hairless pussy. Andrew started to breathe heavily as he watched Faith reach down to touch the bulge in his pants. He scooched his butt up so she could easily undo his belt and pull down his jeans and boxers. His cock sprung up from the elastic in his waistband like a medieval catapult.

10

Faith didn't care how big his penis was. She wasn't planning to enjoy this activity. Mentally prepared for the next act she dropped to her knees at the end of the bed and wrapped her lips around his cock. She took her time sucking on it, while rhythmically bobbing her head and giving Andrew a chance to grow inside her mouth. Andrew meanwhile laid back on the mattress watching her work and loving the attention.

Faith had a talent for oral sex and enough practice to have perfected the art. Feeling that her head performance had been sufficient she rose back to her feet and reached down to pull a condom from her purse. She opened the wrapping and rolled the latex over Andrew's penis with the grace and efficiency of someone who had done this a hundred times.

She then crawled on top of him and slowly lowered herself onto his erection, the lube helping it slide in with ease. Hoping this wouldn't take too long, Faith rocked her hips back and forth while Andrew kept his hands on her thighs. She looked down at his face, made eye contact, and wondered whether or not he noticed her bored expression. This only lasted a few minutes before Faith grew impatient again and slid herself off.

She positioned herself on the bed next to Andrew with a pillow under her belly. The pillow would help keep her ass in the air and it served as another effective cue for Andrew to change positions. He understood his new role and knelt behind her with his cock in hand, slowly guiding it into her and allowing her body to completely engulf him.

Faith moaned when he entered her. Not out of pleasure, but more so from the discomfort. And because she knew it would increase the probability of him busting his nut sooner and ending this part of the evening.

Andrew attempted a few minutes of thrusting before his movements became rigid. Then came the instant relief as Faith felt the reservoir of the condom fill and his cock pulsate inside her. She wished she could enjoy sex with her clients enough to orgasm as well, but it wasn't in the cards. This was all business as usual.

Andrew pulled his dick out of her, now softened but still maintaining some of its girth; the condom wet with the lube from Faith's pussy.

"Very nice," Faith said, rising to her feet.

She found that men liked it when she complimented their skills in the sack. It increased the chances they would call her again for repeat business, which meant a more predictable income. Plus, Andrew had been a friendly one so she wouldn't mind visiting him again.

Andrew pulled the condom off his flaccid penis and threw it in the trashcan beside the bed. He had gotten what he needed and was still enjoying the rush of endorphins and dopamine releasing from his brain. Faith's pussy made him forget his worries and for a moment he started to wonder if he might be falling for her. Despite her drab demeanor, he had a strong yearning to get to know her and find out.

Faith nakedly walked to the bathroom to pee and use toilet paper to remove the excess lube from her used and sore cunt. She didn't bother closing the door. After flushing the toilet, she observed Andrew's collection around the sink. On the counter was a stick of deodorant, a toothbrush, and three credit cards that upon closer inspection belonged to three different people.

The credit cards made her wonder if he was a thief and she suddenly panicked at the thought of him snooping through her purse. She rushed out of the bathroom and was thankful to see her purse still sitting on the floor undisturbed. She looked around the hotel room, now noticing that Andrew's camera was being situated on a tripod next to the bed. Faith was confused by the new setup, but what concerned her more was seeing Andrew use one hand to adjust the focus while the other gripped a 9mm semi-automatic.

3

"Um, what's going on?" Faith asked, her eyes locked on the gun.

"Huh?" Andrew asked, before noticing how off-putting the situation appeared. "Shit, I know this looks weird. I'm a photographer... and I have this gun just in case you turn out to be crazy."

Andrew giggled to lighten the mood. Faith wasn't amused.

"What the fuck are you talking about?" she asked.

"You know," Andrew replied, "in case you or your pimp tried to rob me or something. You can't be too careful. I've met a lot of escorts who would do some psycho shit if given the chance."

"I thought you said this was your first time," Faith reminded him. She wasn't at all concerned about not being his first, but she was still shaken from seeing the gun in his hand.

"Well, sorry to break the news but you're not the first hooker I've been with," Andrew answered, with a newly visible confidence.

Faith knew she shouldn't have been surprised. "That's fine, I really don't give a fuck about that. But I do think I should go now."

"Wait," Andrew protested, "don't we have like 20 more minutes?"

"No," Faith replied plainly, starting to put her clothes back on, "I'm done here."

She had been with some aggressive clients in the past but she'd never been in a situation where one of them could shoot her dead. None that she was aware of anyway. She put on her coat while Andrew secured the gun in his backpack and placed the backpack in the corner.

Andrew was committed to having her stay just a little while longer. "Listen, I'm an artist and photographer. I'm doing a whole piece on women like you and I just want to talk for a few minutes."

Faith wasn't buying it. She put her purse back around her shoulder and slid her feet back into her heels.

Andrew would need to try a different approach. "How about this, I'll give you an extra $200 if you stay another hour."

"No thank you," Faith replied, making her way to the door.

"How about $500?"

This figure got Faith's attention. That was high-class escort money and she wouldn't even have fuck him again or do anything gross. Still, she wanted to make sure she understood the offer. "You're going to pay me $500 just to talk to me for an hour? Are you fucking retarded?"

"Listen," Andrew repeated, "I know this sounds weird, but I swear I'm legit. All I want you to do is tell me about yourself, how you got where you are, and let me take one or two pictures. $500."

Faith thought about it for a moment. This was all crazy, even for her.

Andrew walked over to the desk, picked up his wallet, and pulled out the remaining cash from the bifold. Having only $120 in twenties he picked his duffel bag up from the floor and unzipped it, pulling out a black pouch that served as his personal piggy bank.

Faith's eyes widened seeing the amount of cash in there as Andrew pulled out the remaining $380. There had to have been over a thousand dollars in the black pouch, making her wonder if maybe she should have robbed him after all.

"Alright. Let me get a few things from my car and then I'll talk to you. I'm gonna need to be way more fucked up if I'm gonna tell you about my life," she said.

"I'll walk you out," Andrew replied, being the gentleman that he was.

Now that they were back in the hotel room, Andrew removed his jacket and hung it in the closet while Faith pulled her bottle of

14

Smirnoff out of a plastic shopping bag. She took two swigs from the bottle and offered some to Andrew; a new courtesy since he was paying top-dollar for her time. He refused the drink, instead taking a sip of the Diet Mountain Dew he had sitting on the dresser.

After screwing the cap back on, she took out the clear bag of cocaine and prepared an altar on the bedside table situated between the two queen-sized beds. She poured some out onto the wooden surface near the lamp, bible, and alarm clock, creating what looked to be a little white ant hill. Faith then took out her drivers' license and divided the pile into four individual lines. Andrew watched her work like she was an artist preparing paint on a palate.

Faith looked up to Andrew as he observed her. "You don't mind, do you?" she asked, now feeling obligated to ensure he was comfortable with her getting coked up in his room.

"Not at all," he replied, "make yourself at home."

Faith rolled up one of her hard earned twenty-dollar bills and leaned over to snort the nearest three-inch line. After taking it all in one go, she cocked her head back and sniffled twice, again trying to work the powder past her sinus congestion. Andrew was no longer watching Faith enjoy her vices. Instead, he had shifted his focus on looking through the camera lens and positioning her perfectly into the frame. Faith stared at him judgingly, visibly uncomfortable with having it on her during their little rendezvous.

"I just want a few headshots. I don't need to get any of that other stuff, so don't worry about that," Andrew said, hoping that his words would provide assurance, "let me get a picture right now though. Stay just like that."

Faith remained in her slouched position, her hair and makeup now jostled. She looked like she had just woken up from a hangover as Andrew hit the flash.

"Thank you for that. I'll need a few more as we go on," he said.

"This is getting weirder and weirder," Faith complained. "Are you a cop, or are you trying to put me on the internet or something? Because if you are then I'm gonna need more money."

"No, not at all," Andrew replied, "this is for my own personal collection. I'll tell you what. I'll throw in another $100 if that makes you feel better."

"Alright, whatever gets you off, I guess," Faith agreed.

Andrew had the camera set up and illuminated Faith with the lamp on the bedside table. Faith sat on the bed patiently while he hit the camera's flash button one more time.

He then pulled out a voice recorder from his pocket and set it on the bedside table next to her, just a few inches from her precious cocaine.

"This is Faith," he spoke into the recorder, "she's an escort with a story to tell."

Faith was almost about to tell him to back off from her blow, but he did so before she had to get defensive.

"So, tell me your story. What got you to where you are now?" Andrew asked.

Faith shook her head, still in disbelief that this was happening. She put together a vague response, "Um, my name is Faith. And I'm doing this because I need to live and this fucking city isn't doing me any favors."

"Can you elaborate on that a little more?" Andrew asked, staring at her intently, "tell me about your life growing up. I'm paying you to give me the details."

Faith sighed, unscrewed the cap from the bottle, and took another sip. "God damn. Alright then, here we go."

4

Faith had just turned 16 when she dropped out of Patrick Henry High School. She was having difficulty in each of her classes, and in the end, decided that she already knew all she needed to know about the world.

Life was significantly easier for her when she could drown out the responsibilities and trivial bullshit of teenage being. She could instead spend her time masturbating or fantasizing about what her life would eventually be like. Faith wanted to be an actress living in New York or Los Angeles, and no one ever needed a PhD for that. She wanted to be famous; someone whom people looked up to, someone that others would aspire to be, someone who had made the right choices. Most of all she was hoping for any means to move out of her current stasis. She was just waiting to take the next step to get there.

The problems with school escalated during her freshman year when she met a boy named Ty. He was a senior, gorgeous to look at, and knew how to make Faith believe that everything was going to be okay. Ty had real plans for the future. He was planning to make a career for himself as a DJ, and that was enough for Faith to believe he could be the one to take her away from the dark hole she was living in.

She had been walking out of school to skip 5th and 6th period when she found him doing the same thing. As they both exited through the maintenance entrance, Ty took a break to check out the full figure of a freshman girl, while she saw this as a golden opportunity to smoke a cigarette with a hot guy.

"Hey, do you have another one?" she asked while Ty pulled out a pack of Newports. Faith had her own pack of Marlboro Lights that she swiped from her mom, but saw this as a good way to break the ice.

Ty took another glance at her body then locked his eyes on her baby blues. "I don't have any more on me, but there's another pack in my car. Come on."

The two love birds hung out next to Ty's Mustang chatting, flirting, and laughing together as Faith became smitten with his confidence, muscles, and brown eyes. She stood close by him while he talked about all the stuff he was going to do next year, and even hinted that she could come along with him. As he rambled on about himself, Faith rubbed her breast on his arm, giving the obvious indication that she would be his if he wanted to have her; and he certainly did.

Over the next four weeks she saw Ty nearly every day and remained entranced by the lines he gave her, along with the promises that he would take her places she'd never been. Faith ate up every word. It felt like something wonderful was blossoming, but like all good things, their relationship would have its own sordid twist of fate.

Ty's parents were out of town on their own little vacation, giving him a seamless occasion to throw a get-together with his friends. Faith was apprehensive at first, afraid that she'd have to compete with the older, prettier girls who would undoubtedly trash her. Thankfully for her, she found comfort in seeing that only Ty's male friends showed up to his party.

Faith was having the time of her life. Ty's friends treated her like a princess; pouring her shots of Grey Goose and Hypnotiq, and showing her how to properly do a rail of cocaine. She didn't experiment with the coke this time. Not out of morality, but because she was still scared from all the D.A.R.E. classes she had to sit through as a kid. She wanted to have fun, but she was afraid of overdosing after the first hit and convulsing on the floor in front of her new company. There was nothing sexy about an overdose.

The liquor, however, she consumed in luxury. Faith needed to keep up with the guys to show them that she was better than all the other bitches in the senior class. After all, these weren't typical immature freshman boys that she was partying with. These were practically men, and with their maturity they knew how to make a girl feel special.

Ty kept Faith close to his side whenever he could, holding her by the waist and sometimes grabbing her ass to verify that she was still his girl. He only left her alone to take a piss or step outside to smoke another cigarette. On any other night, Faith would have happily joined Ty outside, but in this moment, she was loving the attention and admiration that she got from the rest of the guys.

She also treasured the sense of power in having something they desired but couldn't get. No matter how much they wanted to fuck her, she wasn't going to let any of them have her pussy. She would have appreciated if they tried though. She was horny as hell.

After two more hours of debauchery, Faith realized that she had taken off her shirt for some reason and was now only wearing a bra. She also noticed that each of Ty's friends had tried to make out with her at least once when he wasn't around. She knew the consequences of cheating, but the more liquor she consumed, the hotter this party became and the more she wanted to be taken by all of them at the same time.

The kisses and hidden entanglements were overwhelming, and while Ty was out smoking his eighth cigarette, Faith found herself in a bedroom that she assumed belonged to his parents. Unsure of how she got there or who she was with, she enjoyed his hands roaming her body and sliding up under her bra. With his tongue in her mouth, she blindly moved her hands south until they reached his dick. She had become an animal in heat, no longer able to comprehend anything other than her lust. Hoping to take advantage of the moment before Ty came back inside, she quickly unfastened his belt and dropped to her knees. Faith couldn't recall his name, but it only took him two and a half minutes to shoot his cum down her throat.

The high school senior looked behind him while fastening his belt, checking to see if anyone had caught him messing around with Ty's girl. Feeling that he was safe, he left Faith on her knees and nonchalantly walked back to the kitchen.

Faith was hooked.

She found that nothing else mattered in the world when someone's orgasm depended entirely on her. The rest of the guys appeared to have talked about what happened, because every so often another one would find her to have his turn. In what felt like a lucid dream she ended up sucking off and swallowing each of the party's attendees one by one. Faith's pussy got wet at the idea of Ty taking her to his bedroom and sticking his dick in her mouth too. Then he'd claim her back by fucking the shit out of her and letting her fall asleep in his arms.

Unfortunately, Ty had caught wind of Faith's behavior over the course of the evening and was going to take his time showing her exactly how it made him feel.

Meeting Ty in his bedroom, Faith had expected him to take his turn with her. Instead of dropping his pants to the floor, Ty let his anger guide his next series of actions.

"Fucking slut!" he screamed, while slamming her against the bedroom wall, bloodying her nose and chipping her front tooth. It was okay though. Through the pain of it all Faith knew this was only temporary. Faith suspected that once he got it out of his system, Ty would return to being the sweet guy she knew and loved; the one who was going to take her away and save her.

Still overcome by his temper, Ty threw Faith onto his bed and pushed her bloody face into the pillow. He then pulled her shorts off and proceeded to fuck her in the roughest, most enjoyable way she'd ever, and would ever be fucked by a man. There was no doubt about it. Faith had found love.

Ty remained distant from her for the remainder of the weekend, only displaying fondness when he was ready to be inside her again. Faith had a feeling that things would never be the same; and on the following Monday he told her at school that he never wanted to see or hear from her again.

News traveled fast that she was the dirty slut who sucked off a whole house of guys in one night. No shame was brought to the seniors who came in a freshman girl's mouth, but the looks she received from everyone in her grade, and the comments she got from the thirsty boys in her classes, made her regret her decisions. That night was the first time in years that she felt good, so it was inevitable that it would fuck things up in some way.

When her parents found out what occurred, they were both furious and embarrassed, but how they treated Faith was of little difference. Not feeling particularly safe at school or home, Faith dropped out of Patrick Henry just before the beginning of her sophomore year. It would be one less thing for her to worry about, and her parents didn't seem to even notice.

Shortly after her 18th birthday Faith got a call from Ty saying that he missed her, and maybe there was hope to rekindle their broken relationship. She had seen already that he was toxic, but she also missed him and cherished the idea of following her heart. Faith still loved Ty and envisioned him as the ticket to a better life. The things he said over the phone penetrated her, and before hanging up she had decided that she'd pack up her things and leave with him that night. Her parents protested her choice when she told them what was happening. They called her stupid, lazy, and immature, which solidified Faith's reasons for wanting to get out of there fast and never look back.

Faith was taking the next steps to a better life, leaving her parents and everyone she knew behind. Ty was a mature 21-year-old now, working as a DJ at Club Velvet in Richmond. It wasn't probable that he'd break her heart again. He promised that they could make a home together. They would just need a little bit of money starting out, but it was destined to work in one way or another.

5

Making enough money for the two of them meant that Faith would also need a job. Not many employers in the city were looking to hire a high school dropout, and she certainly wasn't about to cook fries at a fucking McDonald's. With her lack of social etiquette, she probably wouldn't have much luck as a Walmart cashier either. Thus, her choices were rather limited.

Luckily for her, Ty had a steady job as the resident DJ at Club Velvet. Stripping was never the option Faith had planned for, though it did provide a method for her to get paid in cash.

She was excited once she found out she could get drunk or stoned before each shift; which in turn would help her deal with all the sloppy pricks she'd have to interact with each night. Strip club managers tended to not care what a girl had to do to make her money. As long as her tight ass and bouncing tits kept the clientele coming, and she didn't do anything stupid that would attract the cops, the rest was fair game.

Some of the girls offered meetups, but it wasn't something they would talk freely about in the dressing room. Everyone knew though. Keeping a quiet hustle was the game, but Faith had not yet ventured for work outside the club. For now, she was content dancing to the music, removing her clothes, and giving a lap dance to whichever loser asked for one.

It felt unusual grinding on another man's crotch while seeing Ty in the same room and only a few feet away. He'd sometimes stare at her from the DJ booth, reminding her of the party from all those years ago. Faith's pussy would moisten at the idea of him slamming her against the wall and fucking her viciously. She knew that if she worked hard enough, he'd just might do it

But until that day, Faith would have to wait and deal with her antipathy for all the men who threw money at her on stage. She knew she was just a piece of ass to them and that they were just open wallets for her. There was an odd sense of humor and satisfaction in knowing that she resented them as much as they resented her.

Faith also had an unshakable urge to bitch slap all the other girls she worked with, except of course, for Bethany. Bethany was a chubby brunette with freckles who Faith didn't mind talking to because she was less attractive, and therefore didn't pose a threat. Bethany was also the one who convinced Faith that cocaine was okay in moderation, and doing a couple bumps before work was a good way to get warmed up. Both girls found that their nights at the club were more fun with stimulants, and they could make a hell of a lot more money with the extra energy. The trashy girls smoked meth but the self-respecting ones did coke.

Faith met Bethany on her first night dancing. She hadn't much luck assimilating with the other dancers as they all brushed her off as the new competition, but Beth was different. She was welcoming yet honest, explaining the harsh realities of working in a place like this. Faith would have surely found out on her own, but it was helpful having a friend to guide her in.

Watching Bethany work the floor over the next few months and overhearing her conversations, Faith quickly learned about the real bread and butter of this business. Stripping was good for making a hundred dollars, but meeting a man out in the parking lot could take a girl to the next tax bracket. Ty would never have to know.

Her opportunity to test this theory came during a slow night in June. Bethany was nice enough to introduce Faith to her coke dealer who happened to like the way Faith moved her body on the stage.

"Chloe, get over here!" Bethany called from across the club, "I want you to meet Miles." Chloe was the stage name that Faith chose for herself. Bethany went by Aimee.

Faith strutted her way over to their table while making eyes at the gentleman. "I haven't seen you around here before," she said, sizing him up.

"I'm a busy man. Business never sleeps," Miles responded.

Bethany and Miles continued their conversation as though Faith wasn't there until it was time for Bethany to take the stage. Before leaving she whispered something in Miles' ear. Faith couldn't make out what she said but assumed it had something to do with getting more blow.

"Your girl told me a lot about you," Miles said calmly.

"She tends to do that," Faith responded, not having much else to say. She wasn't really a people person.

"Well, I'm tired of sitting here. Let's go to my car so we can talk." Miles was a man that knew what he wanted.

Ty wasn't there to stop her. He had called out sick, though Faith knew he was just feeling hungover from the previous night. Regardless of his reason, Faith was grateful that he wasn't around to give her a hard time for what she was about to do.

Faith sat in the passenger seat of Miles' Dodge Challenger, curious if she was the one who was supposed to start or if that was his job. Miles slipped her $100 from his wallet and hastily unfastened his belt. Faith watched as he pulled his boxers down and showed her his black cock, the largest that she'd ever seen in person. Ty was half his size and she began to question if she'd even be able to fit it all inside her.

With it being her turn to reciprocate, she leaned over the console and stroked him for a few seconds before going down and taking as much as she could into her mouth. Her head bobbed while she struggled to ignore her gag reflex. She started to wonder if she should have been hooking up with black guys all along. He smelled like cologne and was gentler than she had expected, brushing his hand through her hair while she covered his cock with saliva. Faith started thinking about the guys she sucked off at that party and how immature and stupid they were. It was a stark contrast to Miles. He was a real man.

24

His fingers stroked her pussy through the fabric of her shorts, filling the car with the musty aroma of her aroused cunt. Feeling antsy herself, she took his cock out of her mouth and reached between her legs, pulling her shorts and g-string to the side. She then crawled over and straddled him in the driver seat, slowly filling her void with his anaconda. Faith thought her pussy was going to tear as she rode him with vigor. She didn't care who she was fucking at this point. She loved Ty, but he could never fill her like this.

Faith listened to Miles' groan and felt her pussy overflowing with his seed. She felt the extra lubricant merge with hers while their warm bodies embraced for a brief moment of esteem. The fear crossed her mind that she may have just gotten herself pregnant from this guy, but it faded as soon as she slid off his dick and sat back in the passenger seat.

"Damn girl, you're tighter than I thought you'd be," Miles said.

"Thanks," Faith answered, assuming that was meant to be a compliment.

"I'm gonna go now," he said, hitting the unlock button on his door to signal that it was time for her to leave.

"Okay," she dumbly replied.

On her way back to the club Faith was disconcerted to see Ty waiting for her at the door. She didn't know how long he'd been standing there or who had tipped him off, but she had a feeling that he saw a bit more than she would have liked.

"What the fuck do you think you're doing?" Ty asked, his fist clenched.

"Nothing. We weren't doing nothing." Faith answered, her voice cracking.

Ty slapped her across her face. "You're such a fucking slut!" he shouted before shoving her back.

Faith lost her footing and fell to the ground. She was scared but she'd seen this coming and knew that it was best to just let him finish. Ty kept shouting and kicked her repeatedly until a familiar voice called him from the parking lot.

"Back the fuck off, man!" Miles yelled, running to Ty and pushing him to the side.

"Motherfucker!" Ty screamed back, "first you sell me shitty heroin and now you're fucking my girl? Fuck you!"

25

Ty attempted to throw a punch but missed, leading to the two of them fighting above Faith's body. In a strange way, she found it quite romantic.

They continued sparring until Miles threw a correctly placed right hook that put Ty onto the ground. It would have been a clean knockout if not for Ty hitting his head on the curb, denting his skull, and spilling his blood onto the concrete.

Faith had an array of conflicting emotions watching her boyfriend crack his head open. Some sadness, some embarrassment, some relief. She imagined that Miles could become her new Ty and save her from all this shit, making it so she would never have to strip again. When she got back to her feet, she touched his arm.

"Thank you," Faith said sweetly.

"Don't touch me, bitch," Miles said back to her, leaving her where she stood and walking back to his car.

Faith went back into the club to find Bethany, who was quick to ask how her date with Miles went.

"I think I'm gonna go home," Faith said to her with a listless expression on her face.

"What's wrong?" Bethany asked.

"Nothing," Faith lied, "I just wanna go home."

"Okay, baby. I'll call you later."

Faith walked back outside and relished the cool breeze of the summer night hitting her face.

It was the perfect temperature for a long walk home, so that's what she did, averting her eyes from Ty lying still and quiet on the sidewalk.

Ty never came back to the apartment. Instead, Bethany showed up demanding details of what had happened, asking if she'd talked to Miles, and wondering if Miles knew that Ty was dead. Bethany filled Faith in on what took place after she left, mentioning that Ty was already gone by the time the police showed up; and now Miles wasn't answering his phone. They would both probably have to find a new dealer, which annoyed them, but for now there were more pressing issues at hand.

It was a good thing that Bethany had delivered the news before the landlord could kick Faith out of Ty's apartment. With nowhere to go she thought about the possibility of going back to her parents, but instead decided to take what money she could find and move in with Bethany and her cats.

Over the next two weeks Faith had the opportunity to learn everything she needed to know about being an escort in contemporary America. The internet became their main source of business, working Craigslist during the day and dancing most nights when the money was good.

In spite of the circumstance, this would end up being the best time of their lives. Faith would sometimes feel depressed about that fact, crying at night and knowing that she'd never get to be a real actress. She wondered how long it would be before she caught an STD, and thought about how her life would change if she contracted HIV. She giggled about it, morbidly seeing death by AIDS as a welcoming escape. She would only be so lucky.

6

"So that's how you became an escort," Andrew indicated, as though a lightbulb had just illuminated above his head.

"Yeah, pretty much," Faith said steadily. A long time ago she would have felt some resemblance of shame, but she had already crossed that bridge.

Andrew again stated the obvious. "The more you tell your story the more I'm hearing that your life's been fucked up for a while."

"You could say that," Faith replied.

She took an intermission from the conversation to ingest her third rail of cocaine. Andrew watched the whole process, impressed by how efficiently she could get herself off. He then spent a few seconds trying to figure out how he would phrase the next question.

"So… when did this all start?" was the best he could come up with.

"What do you mean?" Faith asked, stretching out her nostrils with her fingers and inhaling the residue.

"You started your story out in high school, but most high school girls weren't doing the kind of shit you were doing. So, what was it about your life that made you want to do all those things?"

"I was horny and they were hot," she answered simply.

"Come on, there's gotta be more to it than that."

"You don't want to hear about all that shit. And I don't want to talk about it neither," Faith said dismissively.

Andrew continued to pry for an answer that would satisfy his curiosity. "You've come this far; and it's what I'm paying you for, so dig deep. Tell me about your life growing up. It had to have started when you were younger."

Faith looked at the floor. "I still can't believe you paid me money for this. What the fuck's wrong with you? What's this for anyway?"

"I just want to learn about you," he reminded her, "I want to know what happened that made you want to leave your parents and take on this lifestyle." Andrews words were eerily collected.

Faith took another swig from the bottle but didn't bother offering Andrew any this round.

"Alright," she said, "but this is the last one and then I'm leaving. If I wanted to dig up my past like this I'd go to a fucking shrink."

"That's fine. Our hour's almost up anyway," Andrew replied.

Around the time Faith was going through puberty her family would spend a few weekends a year with the in-laws at their river house. While the adults drank margaritas and played board games in the kitchen, Faith and her cousin Sammy played Uno and watched movies in his bedroom upstairs. It was never an enjoyable experience for either of the kids. She was usually bored with the whole endeavor and always looked forward to going home.

One particular night, while their parents were downstairs playing Scrabble, she and Sammy sat on his bed watching Titanic. They laughed at the part with Jack and Rose in the back seat of the old car; feeling rebellious watching a PG-13 sex scene while their parents weren't around. Shortly after Rose's palm hit the fogged class of the car, Faith smiled at Sammy and saw the tent pitching in his sweatpants. She chose not to say anything about it and instead tried to pretend she hadn't noticed.

Faith went back to watching the movie and before she had time to realize what was happening, Sammy had stuck his whole hand up her shirt.

"What are you doing?" Faith asked as Sammy brushed her breasts with his fingers.

Sammy didn't say anything in response, but he looked at her in a way that Faith had never seen before. She was uncomfortable with what was happening, but too nervous to make him stop. Sammy was

29

older, had lots of friends, a ton of video games, and got good grades at school. Everyone, including Faith's parents, said that he was the kind of kid who was going places. So, she didn't want to say or do anything that would make him not like her.

In her brain she was screaming and pushing Sammy away, but her body had betrayed her and started having feelings she wasn't used to. He took his hand out of her shirt and stuck it into her pajama pants, beneath her underwear, and onto her vulva. Faith squirmed, still trying to decide if she liked or hated Sammy for what he was doing.

All she knew for sure was that this was something she didn't want to happen. Sammy took Faith's hand and placed it on top of his tent.

"It's okay. You can squeeze it," he said. Faith froze.

"Faith, we're leaving! Say goodbye to Sammy and come down," her mother Jill yelled from downstairs.

Sammy quickly stood up from the bed, panicking that one of their parents had a clue that he had just felt up and fingered his cousin. Faith did the same, straightening her clothes and hoping also that no one downstairs had suspected anything. Even though she had just been molested, she was more worried that she'd be the one in trouble for it all. Faith took a deep breath and walked toward the door.

"Don't tell anyone about this," Sammy said to her.

"I won't," Faith answered without confidence. She turned back to Sammy. "Don't ever do that again…"

"Okay," Sammy replied. And that was that.

Faith didn't tell her parents about it. Instead, she believed that when she told Sammy to never touch her again that he had listened and would oblige.

She didn't see him again until the following Easter when their families got together again at the river house. Sammy invited Faith upstairs after lunch, but she declined the offer and chose to stay close to her parents this time.

Disappointed, Sammy went into the living room to watch TV, keeping just enough distance from the dining room so he could jump in if Faith started talking about what happened during their previous time together. Faith sat at the table next to her mom and dad and listened to the adults play Yahtzee, smoke cigarettes, and drink Long Island Iced Teas. It all went smoothly until her mom got fed up with her being in the way. The parents were trying to play games and have adult-themed conversations, and having a dumb kid around was making it difficult.

"Why don't you and Sammy go play outside. It's a beautiful day," her aunt Sarah suggested kindly.

Sammy perked up and walked back into the kitchen.

"I think I want to stay here," Faith said.

"Go outside right now, young lady. The grown-ups want to have some fun without you kids," her mother Jill ordered. She tended to be a mean drunk.

Faith looked at Sammy, who looked back at her. He was ready for her to whine or say something stupid, but she was still reluctant to talk about why exactly she didn't want to go outside with him.

The two kids walked on a path toward the river and Sammy tried to make Faith feel more at ease.

"What'd you get for Easter?" he asked, hoping to lighten the mood.

Faith took a few steps to respond but finally did, "Starburst jelly beans, a chocolate bunny, some Peeps…" Her voice trailed off.

They continued walking until they approached the reservoir. Sammy sat on the bench overlooking a flock of ducks and geese swimming. Faith sat next to him without having anything to say. She remembered the feeling of his hands in her underwear and the thought made her tingle.

"Remember the night we watched Titanic?" Sammy asked.

"I don't want to talk about it," Faith quickly replied.

A few minutes later Sammy abruptly stood up from the bench. "Hey, there's a cool boulder over here with paint on it. Let's check it out."

Faith followed. She didn't have any better ideas. She just wanted to get the day over with so she could go home.

31

They walked around the hill behind the reservoir, away from eyeshot of anyone that could be passing by. Faith became tense. She tried calming herself by thinking that nothing would happen that was worse than what had happened before.

"Do you have any homework over Spring Break?" Sammy asked.

"Yeah, I have to read a book and write a-" Faith was caught off guard and interrupted by Sammy grabbing her by the arms and sloppily kissing her lips.

Faith broke from the kiss and tried to push him away. Instead of relenting, Sammy shoved her onto the ground. Faith struggled while Sammy crawled on top of her, kissing her neck, then reaching up her dress to pull down her underwear.

It was the first time her bare vagina had been seen by anyone besides her parents or a doctor. Sammy dropped his shorts to his ankles before wedging himself between her legs. Faith yelled for him to get off, but Sammy had already thought this through and refused to accept her demands. Faith's writhing anger was replaced with pain as she felt his penis penetrate her. She screamed and cried while he tore her hymen and forcefully continued his invasion into her body. She could feel blood trickling out onto the itchy dry grass while the burning pain became unbearable. Feeling like this was going to kill her, she closed her eyes and prayed that Sammy would finish soon.

Faith didn't know if Sammy had ejaculated. After raping her for a few more minutes he decided that he'd had enough and stopped. Faith was reassured that it was over, while still feeling the soreness and burning in her groin. She stood up with Sammy and they both put their clothes back on in silence.

When they returned to the house, they found that their parents had each drank one too many Long Islands. Faith wanted to go to sleep and never wake up again. She walked across the kitchen toward the living room, being stopped by Jill's drunken arm.

"What on earth were you doing out there? Your dress is ruined!" Jill scolded.

"Sorry," Sammy said while walking in behind Faith, "we were rolling down the hill by the river. I didn't think we'd get so dirty."

Sammy's mother chimed in, "Well, you should think next time. You're too smart to be making dumb decisions."

Faith's father Jake, looked at his daughter and shook his head. Jake too was a mean drunk.

Jill stared and scowled. "We're going to have to get it dry-cleaned now. Go wash yourself off. I can't believe you."

Jill went back to her drink while Faith went upstairs alone. Sammy stayed with the adults and opened the refrigerator for something to eat. He was pretty worn out himself.

Faith washed off the dirt from her arms, then found her way to the spare bedroom. After taking off her clothes she threw herself onto the bed, closed her eyes, and started to cry.

7

The ride home was awkward to say the least. Jake was driving because he was usually the one who sobered up first. Jill sat in the passenger seat pensively, still intoxicated, her eyes wandering to the things they passed along the highway. As per usual she'd had too many drinks and would therefore be an insensitive bitch for the rest of the evening. It was a contrast to her usual state of indifference that allowed her husband to berate Faith on a regular basis. Jill was never the protecting mother that her daughter needed; but if Faith had to decide, she'd prefer an absent mother to the vicious one she was sitting in the car with.

"I still can't believe you got your dress all filthy," Jill said.

Faith didn't reply. She knew better than to pick fights with her at a time like this.

Well?" her mother insisted.

"We weren't rolling in the grass," Faith said timidly.

She now had to decide if she was going to tell her parents the truth. Once she made this decision it would be one that she'd have to hold on to for the rest of her life. Still, she had hope in the thought that her parents would be understanding enough to take her side.

"Sammy forced me to have sex with him," and the die was cast.

"What the hell are you talking about?" Jill asked, acid on her tongue.

Faith trembled with her speech. "Outside today. He pushed me on the ground and had sex with me. I didn't want him to."

"You need to cut that shit out, your lies," Jake interrupted. Sammy was his nephew by blood and he wasn't going to tolerate slander.

"It's true," Faith said, starting to tremble again, "and the last time we went over there he touched me and I didn't want him to."

"You're just mad at him for getting you in trouble!" Jake shouted back. Everyone loved Sammy.

Faith was grounded when she got home. No TV or computer time for two weeks. Her anger at being hurt by Sammy and then having her parents not believe her overshadowed the fear that she may now be pregnant or have an STD. She took a shower for nearly an hour trying to wash away the icky feeling, but it stubbornly remained with her. She felt dirty, degraded, and disgusted, but the more she scrubbed the more she started to think that she could actually kill herself and escape the bullshit that she had no control over. She didn't know what she wanted to do. One thing was for sure though. If she ever saw Sammy again, she'd bite his fucking dick off.

It was now summer and she had no interest in going to the pool, or being in any situation where she was wearing fewer clothes and vulnerable. She looked at every boy who passed by, wondering if he would be the next one to attack. The more she felt this anxiety the more her vagina would remember how the sex felt, and that made Faith feel like she couldn't even trust herself.

Home alone while her parents were out shopping, she sat on the couch in her underwear, watching Buffy, and smoking a cigarette that she'd taken from her mom's purse. Watching Spike throw himself onto Buffy made her think again about that afternoon and before she knew it, her body started to react once again. Faith hated thinking about her cousin, but at that moment she remembered the sensation of being filled with him. She slipped her fingers into her vagina and fantasized about someone else taking her, maybe this time without so much pain.

The rest of summer vacation played out with her masturbating every opportunity she had, sometimes multiple times a day. When her fingers no longer gave the same thrill, she graduated to hairbrushes, Sharpie markers, and her electric toothbrush. The pinnacle of her perversion, however, was when she saw her family's mutt Max, licking his crotch and his red penis protruding from the sheath. The next thought to cross her mind was gross, but she was much too horny to be shrewd.

She got off the couch and walked over to the dog, knelt down, and wrapped her fingers around his penis. Max became instantly excited, eyes widened with anticipation for what Faith would do next. Faith removed her underwear and got back down on her knees, pointing her butt toward the canine. Thrilled to join her in the activity, Max instinctively stuck his nose in her crotch, licked a few times, and became enamored by her scent. Faith closed her eyes wondering if this would hurt as badly as when Sammy did it. She wondered if it would always hurt.

Before she could think any more on the matter, Max jumped up, wrapped his paws around her waist and began hitting her in the back of her thighs with his lipstick penis. She flinched as the dog stabbed her backside repeatedly, until she felt the wild sensation of his penis finding its way home.

She screamed at first with the dog's rapid force, feeling him penetrate and fuck her with his beastly lust. In his mind, Faith was just another bitch, but to her she was committing an ultimate taboo by giving herself to this slobbering mutt. The nails on his paws scratched her sides while electricity conjured inside her and spread to every limb of her body, reaching the tips of her toes. Her eyes rolled back as she moaned in ecstasy.

While catching her breath, Faith attempted to pull away from Max, but the dog refused to release her from his grasp. Faith soon felt what seemed like a baseball swelling up inside her. She let out a gasp in shock but was unable to break away from his hold on her. Blood and vaginal fluid leaked out, mixing into a cocktail with the dog's semen on the floor. She tried again at tugging away but it was of no use, and the two of them stood butt to tail with this penis knotted inside her.

Ten excruciating minutes had passed and Faith was still unable to break free. She heard the front door open and her parents calmly walk in, unaware and mentally unprepared to take in what they were about to see.

"Oh my god, what the hell are you doing!?" Jake yelled.

When Jill had her chance to witness the scene taking place, she let out a curdling scream and stormed back outside, wishing to God that this wasn't real.

Faith remained on her hands and knees, sobbing, while fate allowed for the dog's knot to finally deflate and free her. She crawled away mortified; not so much over what she'd just done, but the fact that she'd gotten caught by her parents. Max walked to the corner and licked his genitals while Faith hunched forward and rushed upstairs to her bedroom.

Jill came back inside and joined Faith in her room. She slapped her repeatedly across her face, called her a nasty whore, and reminded her that she was an abomination who would go to Hell for what she had done. The liquor was strong on her breath as she shouted.

In between the sounds of her mother hitting her, Faith could hear Max growling and yelping while Jake repeatedly kicked him. When Jill got tired of condemning Faith, she went back downstairs to join her husband. Faith stood in the middle of her bedroom, thinking about how her life had again hit a point of no return. She locked the door and laid in her bed, listening to her parents discuss downstairs what needed to be done. Both of them agreed that they could never talk about this to anyone.

Faith listened to Jake take Max to the back yard, followed by Jill screaming behind him.

"You're sick, Faith! I can't believe you!" Jill shouted up at Faith's window from outside.

A minute later the blast of Jake's shotgun could be heard for miles. Faith knew what had just happened but didn't want to put the pieces together. She had just had the best sex of her life from a dog, and now that dog was dead because of it. She stayed in her room the rest of the evening with her face pressed against her pillow, imagining how life would be drastically different once she finally made it to New York or LA.

8

"Wow…" Andrew said under his breath.

"Yeah, it's not my proudest moment," Faith replied. She leaned over and snorted the last line off the table. After re-visiting these stories, she felt like she deserved something to take off the edge.

"What were you thinking?" Andrew asked.

Faith did her sniffling routine before answering. "I used to think it was because I was thirsty and craved anything that would take my mind off everything else. But now I think I'm just a fucked-up person with a fucked-up head."

"Did you ever see Sammy again?"

"A few times over the years, usually around Christmas. My parents thought I was lying, but with everything else that went down, they didn't want to spend much time outside the house. I think they were pretty messed up from it too."

"I can imagine," Andrew replied, still thinking about the clusterfuck of a story he just heard. Despite Faith's horrid past, Andrew had developed an even stronger interest in knowing more about her and being the one that could help get her on the right track.

Faith continued, "I think with it all I was just hoping that someone would've taken me away and made me feel not so angry. Nothing they ever did made me feel better though. I wish my parents would have believed me when I talked about Sammy, just like I wanted Ty to rescue me from my parents. Now all I have is Bethany and even she's a flaky bitch."

Andrew paused before his next question. "I have to ask, have you ever thought about trying to make better decisions?"

"Fuck you," was Faith's reply to that, "yes, I've been trying all my life to get out of this, but I've only gotten as far as becoming a prostitute, fucking all kinds of assholes like you, and answering these stupid questions."

"I'm sorry, I really didn't mean anything by it," Andrew explained.

Faith had enough of his bullshit. "Listen, I'm gonna go," she said coldly, standing up from the bed.

"Wait," Andrew protested, "I'm sorry. All I was trying to say is that I think there's hope in you... why don't you stay the night and we can talk about it more tomorrow? We don't have to have sex or anything. Just let me try and help you, or rescue you if that's what you'd prefer."

Faith's anger grew to a boil. "I'm outta here. I hope you had a good time fucking me and listening to all the messed-up stuff I had to go through."

She put her Ziploc and bottle back in the plastic shopping bag she used to carry them in. "I feel like if I keep talking to you I'll end up using your gun to blow my brains out."

"Please don't do that," Andrew pleaded, "I have personal experience. A woman I love died a little over a year ago. I think about her every day."

Faith feigned sympathy with her body language, but refused to stay another minute.

"I'd like to see you again," Andrew said, watching Faith gather her things and head toward the door.

"I'm an escort," Faith said back, "I'll fuck whoever has money for me."

"If I call you tomorrow, will you come over?" Andrew asked.

"You have my number," Faith replied.

Andrew took another snapshot with his camera, capturing an image of her walking out the door.

Faith stepped out into the harsh night at a brisk pace to escape the cold rain. She could sense that Andrew was standing on the sidewalk watching her while she shivered to her car. She purposefully chose to not look back at him. He appeared so dumb and ignorant in the beginning. Like most of the men she encountered, she thought she had him pegged as another stupid sack of shit; sitting in a category with the other incels too inept to talk to a woman they didn't have to pay for.

The windchill blew on her face as she got closer to her car. Relieved that the appointment was over she took a deep breath and inadvertently ingested a small cluster of cocaine that'd been stuck in her nose. Faith smiled with the unexpected rush and remembered that there was always at least one thing she could count on.

The joy was temporary. In a twist of tragic fate that could only happen to her, the plastic bag she carried tore open, dropping the vodka and Ziploc bag onto the wet pavement. The bottle cracked, which she was okay with since there was another one waiting for her at home. The catastrophe here was seeing her precious Ziploc bag open and nearly all its contents pour onto the wet ground, covering the asphalt like a tiny flurry.

"Fuck!" she shouted, squatting to pick up the bag and save whatever remnants she could gather. Granted, there was only a gram left when it fell, it was still $80 worth and after a night like this she was in no mood to call Miles over for a drop-off.

Feeling defeated, Faith got in her car and started the lonely drive home. The twenty-minute trip gave her enough time to think about the strange encounter with Andrew, while also feeling the disturbance of her hidden memories resurfacing to haunt her again. She shivered as she drove and cursed at the noise coming from the faulty car. On the bright side of all this, if there ever was one, she had made a little less than a thousand dollars so she could at least afford to fix whatever the hell was going on with the heater.

Faith thought it might soothe her gloomy mood to check in with Bethany. If nothing else, it would give her a chance to vent about the weird night she just had. The phone rang three times before Bethany picked up. She was obviously stoned, but still able to talk.

"Hey Beth, I'm on my way home," Faith said.

"Shit girl, where've you been?" Bethany yelled.

Faith looked at the clock and realized that she'd been out for over three hours. They had agreed to call each other when they knew they were going to be back later than planned; just in case their date ended up going south. Bethany was more sensitive about it. A few months prior she had met with a client who got pissed that she advertised anal but then told him it would be an additional hundred dollars. A girl has to have standards after all, and if a man really wants to put his dick in a hooker's ass, he should know he'll have to pay a premium.

Bethany's client couldn't get over his disappointment. While fucking her from behind he surprised her by spitting on her asshole and quickly switching the orifice before she could react. She screamed for him to stop, but he held her down and kept on fucking her until he exploded in her rectum.

She told Faith about it after she got home, crying angrily in the bathroom and cleaning the blood from her anus with toilet paper. It wasn't something they could go to the police for, so her only option was to get another man involved. The following morning, she called Miles and he apparently took care of it. Neither of them heard from the guy ever again, and according to Miles, no one else would either.

"This guy was so weird," Faith explained, "after we had sex, he set up a camera and did this crazy interview thing. He kept asking questions about why I'm an escort and how I got here. It was so weird and fucked up."

"Did he pay you for all that?" Bethany asked.

"Almost a thousand dollars, so I guess it was worth it."

"Holy shit, you could take the rest of the week off from the club and have yourself a little vacation. Buy an 8-ball and take a little ski trip even."

"Maybe," Faith replied. "Hey, in speaking of which, my fucking coke poured out all over the street. Do you have any you could give me? I'll pay you."

"Girl," Bethany answered, "Miles just came over and dropped off some good shit. I got weed, coke, and heroin."

"Woah, what the hell?" Faith exclaimed. She was used to the two of them partying with pills, but heroin was a line she didn't think they'd cross.

"Don't worry. I'm not shooting up or anything. I mixed it with some of the coke and I'm feeling fuckin' good."

Faith was going to respond, but her attention shifted after mistakenly running a red light and nearly getting t-boned by a pickup truck. The close call shook her up but she managed to hold her composure.

"I might give it a shot," Faith said, "but hey, I just nearly got hit by a truck so I'm gonna let you go. I'll see you when I get home.

"Okay sweetie, see you soon."

Faith put her phone down between her legs and continued driving into the night, happy that she would soon get to party dirty with her best friend.

9

Faith lived in a small 2-bedroom apartment that she shared with Bethany in the East End. It was at a convenient location being just a few blocks from Club Velvet. Though, she rarely took advantage of the short walking distance.

During the summer, the night air would be a welcomed adjustment from the smell of stale cigarette smoke and ammonia-rich cat piss that filled her apartment. Most of the time though, Faith didn't like being outside her apartment at night. During daylight hours their street looked like any other, with modest and humble apartment buildings, filled with people who had made poor financial decisions. But when the sun went down it became an illicit jungle of crack, gunshots, and streetwalkers.

When Faith first moved in, she made a sincere effort not to look down on the prostitutes that roamed the area, being that she and Bethany were also in the business of renting out their snatches to the next bidder. What set Faith and Bethany apart from the others was that they were "call girls", not common hookers. They were the sort that required men to go online and call the phone number listed on their Backpage ads. Never the type to stand on the corner in search of car dates; and that alone put them at a higher tier in their eyes. They were professionals.

Faith parked her car and speed walked to her building. Two strange men eyeballed her from by the dumpster smoking what she assumed was a rock; although she didn't bother staying out long enough to find out. Wearing a short skirt and a faux fur coat, she knew what she looked like and didn't want to attract any more attention to herself.

She successfully ignored the two men and quietly entered her apartment. Outside of the two cats greeting her when she walked in, everything seemed calm and eerily quiet. Faith assumed that Bethany was taking a shit or something until she noticed that the bathroom door was wide open and the light was off, quickly squashing that theory.

"Beth?" Faith called out to the silent apartment, receiving no answer in return. She walked down the hallway calling her roommate's name again. The cats meowed and followed closely to remind her that their food bowl had been empty all day. Faith made a mental note to take care of that once she figured out what was going on. Maybe she would even clean their litter box as a treat. Anything was possible.

Bethany's bedroom light was on so Faith figured that she'd either passed out or took to masturbating. Still, she wouldn't be able to rest until she knew for sure. She approached Bethany's door and gave it a quick knock. No response. She slowly turned the knob and peaked in.

Through the cracked door Faith could see Bethany lying on her bed in her tank top and pajama pants, but the way she was laying, with her legs dangling to the floor, gave Faith an uneasy feeling in her stomach.

When she fully opened the door and observed the situation, she learned quickly that something dreadfully wrong had happened to her roommate. Three piles of white powder sat on a plate on the bedside table, and near it, Bethany laid her head; her eyes wide open and staring at the ceiling, white foam pultruding from her mouth.

Faith was speechless. She stared at Bethany's overdosed body while instinctively dialing 9-1-1 on her phone. However, she hung up upon realizing that she was in a precarious spot. There she was with her dead roommate, various narcotics, and a wad of cash in her purse. It wasn't an optimal position to be in when the ambulance arrived.

Feeling like she owed it to her friend, she made another 9-1-1 call, this time from Bethany's phone. Not wanting to give herself up, she simply told the dispatcher that Bethany was dead, gave the address, and then sat the phone gently beside the body. She felt relieved that Bethany would soon be taken care of once the police and paramedics arrived.

Faith's primary goal for the hour was to not get arrested. She recalled that her name thankfully wasn't on the lease, so there was no paperwork tying her to the apartment. Sure, someone at work could potentially link the two living together. It wasn't likely though, as most of their colleagues had their own habits and they would certainly avoid talking to the cops if they could help it.

Acting with record speed, Faith threw her clothes into trash bags along with the things she would need for a brief stint on the road - money, credit cards, food, and a case of bottled water. She didn't like the idea of being homeless temporarily, but she'd have to figure out a new living space on a different day. For the time being her only priority was to get the hell out of dodge.

It took four separate trips, but once each of the trash bags had been loaded into her Cobalt, Faith went back inside to take one last look at Bethany's lifeless body. She felt a sudden wave of grief, knowing she'd never get another chance to talk to her again. She would never be able to tell her about the fucked-up men she encountered, or go on that 8-ball ski trip they had planned. Not wanting to risk the same fate she left the coke-heroin mixture on the table and sadly remembered that she only had a pinch or two remaining in her own stash.

The last task on the list was filling the cat bowls with food and water. She patted them both and said her goodbyes, assuming that whoever came in would figure out what to do with them. Faith looked back at the apartment that she'd been living in for the past year and wondered where her next adventure would take her. Hearing the sirens in the near distance let her know she'd have to contemplate on that later.

Driving away from the building, Faith passed an ambulance speeding to the apartment with its entourage of police cars. Checking off that box in her head, Faith presumed that the problem was handled and she wouldn't need to think on it anymore that night. Bethany and Ty were both gone, there was nowhere for her to go, and she definitely wasn't going to stay with Miles.

She considered getting her own motel room and rejected the idea as soon as it crossed her mind. A motel would most likely require her to put down a credit card, and she much preferred to avoid a paper trail on a night like this. She also thought about the possibility of sleeping in her car. However, she wasn't ready to settle that low just yet. Her paranoia and the crackheads by her apartment had reminded her that the world was not safe. Someone was always out there ready to rob her, or fuck her in one way or another.

Faith ruminated for a few more minutes while putting miles between her and Bethany's corpse. Her mind went back to Andrew and the repulsive interview she had with him less than two hours prior. She didn't like the idea at all, but the more she thought on it, the more he seemed to be the most viable option. He acted like he was trying to help, even when he was being a creep. The question though was that if she called him, would he be willing to let her spend the night without trying to put his dick in her, or worse, ask even more annoying questions?

Fuck it, she thought, picking up her cell phone.

"Hello?" Andrew answered.

"Hey, it's me Faith," she greeted. In her heart she wanted to tell him how horrible her night had been, how she lost her drugs, and how everything had gotten progressively worse. "Listen, I know this is weird, but is it okay if I stay with you tonight?"

"Wow," Andrew replied, "I didn't expect you to ask so soon. Yeah, I can save you tonight."

He was once again acting weird. Faith cringed, wishing he would cut that shit out.

"Alright, I'll be over in a few minutes… we're not having sex again though, and I'm not going to talk about my past either. Maybe we can just watch TV or something."

"Of course. Come on by. I'll hold the side door open for you."

47

"Okay, I'll be there in a few minutes."

Faith ended the call and looked at herself again in the rear-view mirror. The freezing night complemented her need to find a safe, warm, and dry place to stay. Thinking back, she wished she had asked him to book a separate room for her since he had plenty of money for it, but she didn't want to call him again.

It had already been settled. She was going to have to see this asshole again.

10

The carbon steel of the barrel left a metallic taste on his tongue. Andrew had stuck the 9mm in his mouth just to see how it would feel. Suicidal ideation was nothing new for the boy. He would often entertain the thought while in bed late at night, imagining what people would say at his funeral.

His mother would say she should have hugged him more, his peers would say they should have gotten to know him better, and all the girls would say how it was sad that they never gave him a chance. He felt warmth in the idea that he would be appreciated after his death.

Being a kid had been rather difficult for Andrew. He was considered by most of his peers as a weirdo, and was picked on for his weight and odd behavior. After seeing the news footage covering the shooting at Columbine High School, Andrew became obsessed with the prospect of staging his own massacre and making everyone pay for how they treated him.

He hadn't figured out the logistics of how he'd ever pull it off, but just the thought of it gave him a thrill. He liked to visualize putting everyone who ever wronged him into a line and then mowing them down with machine gun fire, grinning from ear to ear as they became a bloody pulp on the ground.

Andrew took the gun out of his mouth and flipped it over to study the trigger assembly. He fantasized about going to campus with it and shooting all the motherfuckers who made him feel like he wasn't good enough to be near them; all the teachers who said he was a bright kid but would fail if he didn't start applying himself; all the girls who would say he was sweet but only saw him as a friend.

He didn't want a friend. He wanted someone to fuck. And all the bitches he imagined naked were too stupid to see him as anything more than a nice guy.

Andrew opened the chamber of the 9mm, clearing it for the hundredth time. He stuck his finger in the barrel, envisioning the bullet shooting out and traveling 1,360 miles per hour to its living target.

Distracted by the increased blood flow to his penis he placed the gun back in its lockbox and returned it to the closet where Judy had kept it hidden. His mother Judy hadn't noticed his frequent visits to her upstairs closet. Like any 20-year-old waiting for their parents to leave so they could jerk off, Andrew waited to be alone so he could satisfy himself in multiple ways.

Internet porn was once his remedy for soothing a painful afternoon, but after months of CNN focusing on Eric Harris, Dylan Klebold, and the Trench Coat Mafia, Andrew started making visits to the gun part of his solitary ritual. It helped tremendously when Judy started working late shifts at the hospital. It gave Andrew plenty of time to take care of himself.

Andrew's dad had left without saying goodbye. Judy at least got a note stuck to the refrigerator which she kept to herself. Andrew had asked about what it said, but Judy was adamant about keeping it ambiguous.

"He doesn't want to be with us anymore," she would say, "like usual, he'd rather be by himself doing his own thing."

Andrew looked for sadness in her eyes whenever she talked about his dad, but most of the time they would display an expression of bitterness and shame. He wondered if he'd ever see him again. Even though he was never the father figure Andrew wanted him to be, he was still the only father he had. Other kids in the neighborhood at normal dads who took part in their lives, cooked on the grill, and showed happiness or anger depending on their day at work. Not him though. He was the dad that glued himself to the TV every night during the week, and on the weekends, he would spend his time alone, usually in the garage or running "errands". Judy would get upset that they weren't spending time together as a family. She'd try to guilt him and Andrew into going out with her, but it was effectively implied that both men of the house preferred to be left alone in their filth.

Then one day, he was gone.

Andrew was confused and felt that his father's departure should have been prefaced with a "your mother and I have been talking" conversation, or at least an explanation with him saying that he still loved Andrew, but had to leave because it wasn't working out with his mother. Anything would have sufficed, really. But instead, the only thing left of him was his gun, bullets, a few shirts, and a series of questions that would forever go unanswered.

Without these answers, Andrew would have to lay in bed at night and wonder what could have been different to make his father want to stay. Then, maybe life wouldn't need to be as turbulent as it was.

Once the divorce settled, Judy tried her best to help Andrew feel like the new man of the house. She gave him more cleaning responsibilities and told him frequently that their awful situation wouldn't last forever. Even though she was being nicer to him, Andrew knew he was only a placeholder until a new man entered her life. It was difficult for him to assert his dominance in the household anyway. Judy had the job and the salary, and Andrew was a community college loser with a near-constant erection. Despite his inadequacy, all he ever wanted in their relationship was for his mother to see him as the testosterone of the family, respect him for that, and maybe suck his dick every once in a while. Unfortunately for him, he would get no such attention from her or from any of the other sluts at school.

When he came home from class one day, he saw his mother in the kitchen crying while cooking dinner over the stove.

"What's wrong with you?" he asked.

Judy paused for a second, working up enough self-control to speak, "I just have a lot going on right now."

She turned her back to him and continued cooking. Andrew didn't know what her problem was, but it was obvious that she needed his love. He walked up to her and embraced her with a hug. He was surprised when she instantly started hugging him back. Feeling her tits press against his chest, Andrew couldn't help but feel his penis stiffening.

He thought that poking her in the belly would awaken some kind of primal lust, but rather than addressing it she simply backed off and went back to preparing dinner.

Andrew took this as a sign that things had become too abnormal for her, so he left his crying mother in the kitchen and made his way upstairs. He never found out exactly what was bothering her.

Back in his bedroom, Andrew turned on the computer and started browsing through his collection of pornography. It was the fastest way for him to subside his anger and depression incurred from a long day. He watched women get fucked and pretended that they were the girls from school who smirked at him. Andrew's animosity and desire for carnage blended with his sexuality, and soon they were both explored in tandem.

Over time he had reached a point where mainstream pornography was no longer enough to satisfy his urges. This in turn began his eternal struggle for something harder. He experimented with MILFs and hentai before eventually graduating to bestiality, incest, and sexual assault – his personal favorite. What started with BDSM opened a rabbit hole to pictures and videos of women being tortured.

While burning the midnight oil, deep in research, Andrew found a website showing videos of real women getting raped. He didn't believe it was authentic at first, but the more he watched, the more he picked up that these weren't staged videos. He was actually having the pleasure of watching these cunts taken against their will; their cries intensifying Andrew's orgasm as he jerked off.

When Andrew wasn't watching porn, he obsessed over the sexual nature of everyone around him. Walking the hallways at school, he tried to be inconspicuous when he stared at a girl's tits, hoping to see her nipples poking through her shirt. If he was feeling artistic, he'd take a good creep shot of their asses when they bent over a desk, or their cleavage when they reached into their book bags. He also took photos of numerous unsuspecting women at gas stations, shopping malls, and especially swimming pools, adding to the ever-growing spank bank on his hard drive. He would look at the pictures when he got home and wonder who these women really were and how well they could suck a dick.

On this particular occasion, Andrew stroked his penis to the image of a blonde older woman in her 40s being taken from behind by a cop, security guard, or whatever. The video shared the screen with a picture of a similar looking woman that he spotted earlier in the week at K-Mart.

She wasn't the most attractive of his collection, so Andrew had difficulty with her at first. But he persevered and kept going until his toes curled and a warm stream of cum had shot onto his belly.

Every woman Andrew passed was no longer a real person, but rather a character in one of the scenarios he fabricated in his head. Sometimes he would masturbate multiple times a day to the thought of them, only stopping when his penis started to sore and become bruised. He knew it was time to call it quits when he started to shoot only tiny spurts of semen. His testicles just couldn't keep up with the immense workload he forced upon them. Nevertheless, he persisted.

When he was alone, Andrew could disassociate from the world around him. Over time he began to have difficulty separating his fantasies from reality. The real world was against him, but he was determined to create the environment and future that that he wanted. A world where he was confident with his successes and women would strive to be around him. This was the goal. This was how he was going to save himself.

11

Three hours had passed. Andrew sat in front of his computer fully naked, having gazed at over two thousand pictures that he'd saved on his computer for inspiration. As he stroked his cock, his anger developed against each of the women in the pictures. They had all probably slept with multiple men, but they would never give him a chance if he tried. He started to wonder if he'd ever get to have intercourse with a woman.

Frustrated again, he decided that it was time for him to lose his virginity once and for all.

He thought that his first sexual encounter would feel more special if he shared the experience with someone he loved. Andrew crept across the upstairs hallway to his mother's bedroom and tried to turn the doorknob, remembering that she had started locking her bedroom at night for some reason.

Unwilling to give up on the mission, or wake her by knocking, Andrew used a bent wire hanger to pick the lock and grant himself access to Judy's sweet domain. She was lying in her bed without a bra on, allowing the moonlight to cast a cool soft glow over her breasts. Andrew stared at her for a moment in this state, feeling a sense of admiration for her. Encouraged by his lust, Andrew slid into his mother's bed and slowly peeled the covers back, surprised to find out that she was sleeping in the nude.

Not wanting to waste any more time with foreplay, he gently spread her legs apart and crawled between them. His erection stood at full attention and homed in on the musty pheromones secreting from his mother's vagina. Andrew shifted himself up her body with his penis in hand and slowly guided it through the mound of pubic hair. Once perfectly aligned, he put his hands on either side of her and slid the entirety of his member into her dry cunt.

Judy woke up immediately to the intrusion, feeling both surprise and sheer terror. It took a few seconds for her eyes to adjust to the darkness and find out who it was on top of her, screaming even louder once she realized it was Andrew. She was unable to believe that her own son was forcing himself upon her. Andrew didn't let her fury distract him. He continued pumping his dick in and out of her, picking up speed as Judy began to lubricate against her will.

"Fuck, Andrew, get off of me! Stop!" Judy cried, trying to push Andrew's sweaty body off her.

"I need this, Mom," Andrew said in between pants.

Judy yelled, slapped him, and scratched her nails into his skin. After watching this kind of pornography for years, the apprehension against him turned Andrew on even more. This had to be love.

Unable to stop him, Judy grew tired of fighting and laid there listless, waiting for it all to be over.

Meanwhile, Andrew was breathing heavily and loving every moment of their connection. He leaned over to nibble on Judy's right nipple but she slapped him away before he could have the chance. The sudden defense from his mother made him for a moment question her intentions.

"Why are you just laying there? Fuck me, baby." Andrew said gracelessly.

"I hate you," Judy muttered.

Her words cut him, but he chalked it up as her having trouble understanding that this was going to make their lives so much better. He started thrusting into her again as Judy laid there closing her eyes.

"I can feel it, Mom. I'm about to cum," Andrew moaned.

"No!" Judy protested.

Andrew's words had awakened something primal in Judy and ignited the fight in her once again. She tried to slide from under him, but the weight of his body kept her pinned to the mattress. Unable to use her physical strength to lift Andrew off of her she started to scream.

"Help! Someone! I'm being raped!" she shouted at the top of her lungs. Andrew tried to shush her and worried that someone outside might get the wrong idea.

"Shut the fuck up. Someone might hear you." he scolded at her.

Judy continued to call for help. Seeing that there was only one real option, Andrew put his hands over Judy's throat and squeezed, silencing her immediately, and reminding him of the women who got choked out on the internet. She tried to pry his hands off her neck, desperately attempting to breathe, but Andrew was too strong and too much in the throes of passion to notice that she was losing consciousness. He kept fucking his mother, each stroke bringing a wave of tranquility as he imagined this being the moment that she would see through his perspective.

With one more intensive thrust, Andrew's body tremored and several waves of semen erupted from his penis into Judy's bleeding vagina. It felt like the biggest load he'd ever shot. Andrew instinctively grunted while tightening his grip on his mother's neck.

"Oh fuck, Mom. That was amazing." Andrew said, catching his breath.

He took his hands off her neck and slid himself out of her, allowing the excess cum to spill out. Judy laid there quietly, unmoving, while Andrew rose from the bed. When he looked down at his mother, he saw that she was peculiarly still, which he thought was strange considering how good she had just been fucked.

"Mom," he asked, "you alright?"

Judy remained silent and motionless. Andrew stared at her and started to become more anxious, fearing that something was terribly wrong with this picture.

Andrew began to hyperventilate in correlation to his elevated heart rate. He tried to shake Judy out of it, hoping that she'd come back any second, but despite his best efforts she remained unresponsive. Her skin was still warm, but her heart and lungs had retired. Andrew checked for a pulse and tried to perform CPR, having no clue how to properly do it. He pumped her chest five times and then put his lips against hers, attempting to breathe life into her lungs and revitalize her body. It was of no use though. She was gone.

He felt a stab of guilt, realizing that he had accidentally murdered his own mother while in their moment of desire. Almost as quickly as the thought came to him, he rationalized that this was all truly an accident, and if she hadn't tried to push him off and scream then none of this would have happened. He started to feel spiteful toward Judy for making him do this.

Andrew sat at the foot of the bed thinking about the events that unfolded and what his next steps should be. Someone would probably wonder what happened to her when she didn't show up to work, and they would undoubtably raise Hell when they found out she had been killed. Andrew feared for his safety and assumed that no one would believe it was all unintentional. He was just trying to make things better for himself, and like all other factors of his existence, it all came crashing down on him.

He had to find a way to get Judy out of the house, understanding that the two of them would never be able to return. That was the only way that Andrew could save himself from spending the rest of his life in prison.

Andrew paced the room while organizing a master plan. Once it came to him, he felt a surge of adrenaline and went straight to work. He started by wrapping his mother in the sheet she was lying on in the same way a person would roll a joint. The sheet was stained with semen, blood, and shit which disgusted him, but he managed to push through it. He tried lowering her to the ground gently before dragging her from her legs out of the bedroom. Bringing her downstairs proved to be difficult as Andrew watched her head hit each step on the way down.

"Sorry, Mommy," Andrew said softly, still feeling a little remorseful over the whole choking business. Now that the body was downstairs, he would need to figure out a plan to get her outside. He first checked to make sure his neighbors weren't around and that no one would see him dragging a large rolled up sheet onto the driveway.

After making some space in the back of their Jeep Cherokee he bent down to pick her up, grunting and struggling with her deadweight. Straining himself to lift her into the trunk he was finally able to fit her in, while making sure that her body was still completely hidden with the sheet.

Now that the most difficult part was over, Andrew roamed the house gathering clothes and food to last him a while on the road, or until he figured out what to do next. He wasn't sure where he was going or how long he would be out, so he thought it best to prepare for the long haul. He brought Judy's purse and all the money he could recover, making $72 total. He then made sure to also grab his camera and equipment, as well as the gun and boxes of ammunition that had been sitting in the closet for years. Playing with that gun was his coping mechanism, so it felt suiting for it to accompany him on the next chapter of his life.

While driving eastward, Andrew wondered if there was anywhere nearby where he could find sanctuary. There was no destination in mind yet and the more he thought about it, the more he felt like Dustin Hoffman in the last scene of The Graduate – the one where he and his girlfriend get on the bus all excited, but then scowl when the truth hits them that they have no idea what they're going to do. For now, Andrew would continue traveling with Judy and try to make do with his wits and the money in his pocket.

12

It had been two days and Judy's body was starting to make the interior of the vehicle reek. It also didn't help that Andrew's sweat and farts joined in with the medley of foul odors. This wasn't a lifestyle he could see himself living in for much longer.

By the time he was two-thirds the way across Montana he knew that something had to change; and it broke his heart knowing that Judy was going to have to leave the picture.

He was luckily able to steal a shovel from an unlocked shed off the highway that he could use to give his mother a proper burial. Andrew took Judy to a secluded place in the hills and started digging. The work was strenuous, but he remembered that this was a service for the woman who had taken care of him his whole life. By digging this grave, Andrew felt that he was becoming a man who took care of business.

He had only dug three feet before his arms became too sore. Feeling tired and winded, Andrew rolled Judy's body into the hole and laid her into a fetal position. He would have preferred to have given her a typical rectangular grave, but he was already feeling weak and they were losing sunlight anyway. There was also the risk that someone would find him and it would be terribly difficult explaining this situation. He didn't expect anyone to understand.

Andrew returned to the interstate feeling broken, yet relieved now that he had one less thing to worry about. There was enough money to last him a couple tanks of gas, but he would have to find some way to make it work beyond that. He thought about his camera and the potential that he could make a living as a photographer. Unfortunately, that dream would take time to grow and he needed resources much sooner than later. In order to survive in this world, he would need to wander as a vagrant, or a traveling freelancer as he liked to call it. Andrew was going to do something with the time he had left, and he was determined to make it work.

By the fourth day on the road, he had made it to Rapid City with only $12 remaining in his pocket. Sitting inside a diner next to a gas station at 1:30 in the morning, eating hash browns and drinking coffee, he somehow attracted the sympathy of the young chubby waitress. She wasn't his type; too many pimples and bad teeth, but he saw her as the chance to possibly get his dick wet and maybe score some extra money.

"I haven't seen you around here before," she said to him, refilling his cup.

"I'm just passing by. Long road trip," Andrew replied.

"Oh darn. Well, you're a cutie so you can come in here any time you want," the waitress said with a flirtatious smile.

Her charming attitude was obviously the method she used to get bigger tips, but Andrew ran with it and let himself become infatuated with the waitress. His eyes followed her as she went about her rounds, becoming angry toward the other men she poured coffee for. They had had their exchange and she was clearly asking for him to help her. She was probably doing this job because she lived in a dirty apartment in a bad part of town. Maybe college had not worked out and she had a mean ass boyfriend who punched her in the face on nights that she came home smelling like cigarette smoke and frying pan grease. She just needed for someone to come in and take her away from all of this misery.

Just before she turned again toward his table, he pulled out his camera and took a quick picture of her backside. He wanted to have this moment saved so he could one day show it to her on their tenth wedding anniversary.

"No rush, but do you want me to clear these plates for you?"

60

"Sure. Hey, what's your name?" Andrew asked.

"Sarah," the waitress replied while gathering the plates and silverware, subtly noticing the camera now sitting on the table pointed at her

"Could you maybe stay here for a little while?"

"Um, not really. It's busy and I'm the only server tonight."

"Okay" Andrew said, watching her clear the rest of the table.

"I'll be right back with your check, sweetie," Sarah said, taking his dishes to the sink.

Though she had dismissed him, he could see in her body language that she loved being filmed and wanted nothing more than for Andrew to be her man. After giving her the last of his money he walked outside, wondering what he was going to do now that he was completely broke and in the middle of South Dakota.

Andrew sat in the parking lot, feeling sorry for himself, yet delighted in the idea that Sarah could take the place of every girl who had ever broken his heart. He held onto his camera, looking through the peephole at the waitress while she cashed out the rest of her customers and sent them on their way. He imagined what she was thinking, zooming the lens on her while she moved from table to table. She wasn't as attractive as he would have hoped for, but his penis started to swell at the thought of her kissing it.

While the two cooks were finishing up their cleaning chores in the kitchen, Andrew watched Sarah walk out of the diner to the parking lot. As she unlocked the door of her dented Nissan Sentra, she got the sudden irk that someone was approaching behind her.

"Hey," Andrew called, startling Sarah and making her step back.

"Jesus! Don't sneak up on me like that!" she spoke out of character, "what's up?"

Andrew took his time putting his words together. "We didn't have a chance to talk earlier. Maybe we could go out and..." Andrew stopped talking after seeing Sarah shake her head. It was already clear she didn't know what was best for her.

He continued, "Listen, I know you're unhappy. So am I. That's why I think we can make each other feel better." He took two more steps toward her. "Come on, I'll make everything right."

"Okay, you need to get the hell away from me," Sarah ordered, sticking her car key between her index and middle finger.

Andrew didn't leave. He instead moved in another three feet, closing the gap between them. "You don't understand. I can help you."

"Back the fuck off, asshole!" Sarah shouted, pushing Andrew back with her free hand.

Andrew grabbed her by the wrist and pushed her against the car. "I'm just trying to help you, bitch!" he screamed, "I'm gonna save you from this bullshit life you're living. Just believe me!"

"Help! Someone, help!" Sarah screamed.

Andrew put his hand over her mouth while she attempted to escape. Sarah kneed her attacker in the groin, which was uncomfortable, but she had missed his balls so he didn't yet have the motivation to comply with her wishes.

What did stop him was the attention she was getting with her noise. Andrew looked over to the diner in time to notice the two cooks catching sight of what was happening and rushing to the door. Unable to claim his prize and realizing that Sarah was just another cunt, he let go of her wrist and reached in his jacket pocket for the 9mm.

He had never shot anyone before, but this time it was the bridge that needed to be crossed. Without putting another second of thought into it he pointed the gun at her belly and pulled the trigger, grabbing her purse from her hands as she fell to the ground. The cooks froze after hearing the gunshot and ran for cover behind the counter. Before allowing anyone else to get a good profile of him, he looked down at Sarah while she laid on the ground crying and bleeding to death. Andrew sulked at her and shook his head. He was disappointed that she didn't give him the chance to show her how nice he was, and as a result she was going to die just like his mother.

Andrew drove his Cherokee deep into the night, recollecting the events that took place at the diner. He looked into the purse he stole from Sarah, seeing over a hundred dollars in cash and several credit cards that he could use as soon as he got another chance to stop. Despite the lack of sex from the pimply waitress, he now had enough money to last him a little longer. He had never robbed or shot anyone before, but the past week had provided many firsts. He smiled while looking at the stars, feeling like things were going to shape up well for him.

13

Andrew drove through Cincinnati, the Cherokee's console stuffed with money and credit cards, and his backseat full of luggage and supplies that he had picked up along his travels. When he observed his setup through the rear-view mirror, he felt accomplished in having created this eccentric bohemian lifestyle, with his entrepreneurial spirit giving him enough income to live by. He was driving across state lines, robbing people, and feeling like a modern-day Bonnie and Clyde, sans the Bonnie. He wanted a partner to take along with him. He would just need to find the right one.

Since shooting Sarah in Rapid City, Andrew had become more comfortable with his weapon. He found that he had a talent for robbing women at gunpoint, grabbing them by the tits, and watching them cry while he put the barrel to their forehead. He knew he'd have to pull the trigger if they attempted anything brave. That was only a rare occurrence, fortunately, and Andrew had exactly what he wanted by the time they started begging for their lives. It wasn't as good as sex, but it gave him the satisfaction he needed.

He had another opportunity to use it while driving through Indiana the previous night.

Stopping at a CVS twenty miles east of Indianapolis, Andrew was interrupted by the family who owned the Honda Odyssey he was breaking into.

"Excuse me! What do you think you're doing?" the husband and father shouted while approaching from the store, his family just a few paces behind him.

Andrew considered explaining that he had found that families with minivans tended to be haphazard with where they put their valuables. But he regrettably didn't have time to make conversation.

The man was bold enough to try and stop him, but quickly found his mistake when Andrew pulled out the 9mm to show that one wrong move would be the end of him, his wife, and their two bitch daughters.

While pointing the gun at each member of the family he couldn't help but feel a spark of arousal, staring at the woman's full figure and the perky bodies of her daughters. He thought about the joy he would have with them as hostages, using them to his delight before painting the side of the highway with their brains.

But now was not the time for that. Andrew only wanted to complete his break-in and move on to the next location; and these assholes were standing in the way.

"Listen man, I'm sorry. Please. I have my kids here," the man pleaded.

Andrew sneered at him, mentally orgasming over the power that he held. Knowing that it would lead to trouble if he was identified, he felt satisfied with his loot and backed away, keeping his eyes on the petrified family. Once there was enough distance between the parties, Andrew turned and ran toward his Cherokee parked by the dumpsters at the Subway across the street. Andrew grew paranoid that one of the security cameras had caught him or his license plate so he thought it best to leave immediately.

While he drove back onto the highway, he looked at the family that he'd just stuck up, hoping they were happy that their lives had been given back to them. He saw the women crying and hugging each other, while the man angrily called the police on his cell phone.

For a novice, Andrew was impressed with himself in this new life of crime. If he couldn't get the sexual gratification that he craved, he felt just as worthy having lethality over people. The look in that father's eyes when he realized that he no longer had control in the situation, that he was talking to a man who had the capability of murdering his entire family, it gave Andrew a sense of temporary sanity. He was finally the one who had the power and he never wanted to give it up again.

Stopping for gas outside of Pittsburgh, he noticed a small massage parlor in the shopping center next door. The older East Asian woman standing outside captivated Andrew so much that he felt compelled to take a picture of her from the gas station. Having never received a massage before, he walked toward the building wondering if this was the type of place where he could get a coveted happy ending. The woman outside glanced at him with an expressionless look on her face and walked inside the establishment.

"How long?" she asked less than five seconds from Andrew entering.

"Um, I don't know. An hour, I guess?" he replied, nervous for no reason he could think of.

"Sixty dollars," the woman said without missing a beat.

Andrew opened his wallet to reveal a thick stack of cash that caused the woman's pupils to dilate. He gave her the money and was led to a low-lit room with a rose lying on the massage table.

"Undress and make yourself comfortable," she said just before leaving him alone in the room.

Andrew was still unsure what to expect in this encounter or exactly what he was supposed to do. He stripped nude and laid face down to await further instructions.

A few minutes later the woman came in and without speaking, started to massage his back and shoulders. The whole exchange was relaxing, giving Andrew time to think about what kind of person this woman was. Did she always live in the United States and decide to open up a business, or is she one of those human traffic victims here against her free will?

As she rubbed his thighs and playfully cupped his balls, he stopped thinking about the trivial nonsense and allowed himself to thoroughly enjoy the blood flow to his penis. A half hour into the massage the woman stopped rubbing and signaled for Andrew to flip around, revealing his erection that pointed directly at her. She giggled and pointed at it, before looking at him and making a hand job gesture. Andrew nodded and she immediately got to work, stroking it gently and only stopping to pull her tits out from her bra. Andrew grabbed the one closest to him and squeezed.

Seeing this as an ample opportunity for more than he paid for, he brought his hand down and slid into the back of her yoga pants, gripping her ass. She let him get a feel for a few more seconds before stepping back and playing her next round of charades. She acted out a thrust with her hips while raising her eyebrows to silently ask Andrew if he would like to fuck her.

Despite this being a monetary transaction, Andrew had never fucked, or so much as touched a woman who wasn't ineffectively trying to fight him off.

It took some mental gymnastics, but he was able to convince himself that this was affection from a woman, just like he'd get from anyone at a bar, or through a friend, or at a coffee shop. The masseuse pulled a condom from her bra and rolled it onto his cock. She then reached under her skirt and pulled her underwear down to the floor. Andrew stood behind her while she positioned herself, leaning over the massage table and lifting her shirt up to expose her spinner ass and lube-filled pussy.

Andrew crouched and stuck his dick inside her. The woman trembled and braced herself against the table while he rhythmically pounded her from behind, heaving, and rubbing his body over the perfumed masseuse. He wanted her to moan for him, but she remained mostly silent, just breathing and waiting for him to finish. Feeling kinky in the moment and wanting to try something new he, cupped her ass cheeks and rubbed his thumb over her anus. She immediately stood upright, forcing Andrew's cock to slide out, and shook her head at him. For a woman selling her pussy for cash she was not into anal, and Andrew wasn't the one who was going to break that spell.

As quickly as she set her boundary, she recognized that he was still a paying customer and resumed her position over the table. Andrew stuck his dick back in her but it didn't feel the same.

That recent exchange reminded him that this was all transactional and without feeling. He could no longer convince himself anymore that she was a woman interested in him, or that she craved his cock.

While Andrew edged closer to ejaculating, he saw the masseuse as another whore who didn't appreciate him the way he deserved. Feeling hate in his heart he continued thrusting into her, now pulling onto her hair and forcing her head to swing backwards.

"No! No!" she yelled, while Andrew grabbed her face with both hands and inadvertently stuck his fingers into her eye sockets. She let out a shrieking scream that sent Andrew over the edge and forced him to fill the condom with his pearl jam. He moaned and grunted with each burst, singing a duet with the woman's painful screams and cries. Worried again that the wrong people would overhear them he pulled his fingers out of her bloody eye sockets and wrapped them firmly around her neck.

With his penis softening inside her Andrew continued to squeeze, only releasing his grip once her body had become limp, either from unconsciousness or exhaustion. Satisfied with his post-orgasm afterglow, Andrew let the masseuse fall onto the ground, now worried that she could wake up eventually and call the police for attempted murder.

He pulled the gun out from beneath his jeans that were neatly folded in the chair. He stopped himself before taking aim, remembering that the bark of the shot would alert everyone outside. Needing an alternative, he held the pistol by the barrel and hit her continuously across her head until there was enough blood protruding from her skull that he presumed she'd never wake up. It truly is a gift to be able to die in one's sleep.

Now fully dressed, he stepped out of the massage room and checked for anyone nearby that could potentially identify him as the parlor's latest customer. No one was around except for the sorry son of a bitch walking across the parking lot, hoping to get his dick rubbed by a woman who had just retired from the business. Not having much time to hang around, he took the $188 and change from the register and left, quietly passing the new customer on the way.

Andrew watched the man in the parlor ring the bell on the counter to get someone's attention. He laughed at the confused man before shifting gears and peeling out of the parking lot.

14

Andrew found that he liked hookers the most. They were down to the point and their lives were worthless enough that he believed he offered more value than he was getting in return. He hoped to find the one who would tell him their story and give him a reason to love them, but if they were unworthy or unable to be saved, then he found solace in removing them from the roster of street trash. This was his new purpose in life.

It started with the streetwalking type; the ones that looked like they would do anything for a rock. Their hair frazzled and their makeup cheap, Andrew had his chance to fuck them in the alleys or in the back of his Cherokee; though, he usually opted for a blowjob from these women. He wanted their pussies, but with the high potential of catching an infection from these whores he didn't want to play Russian Roulette. His life was already chaotic. The last thing he needed were itchy red blisters on his penis and balls, or to go a week pissing razor blades and dripping white goo.

He also worried that streetwalkers would be more likely to attract police attention, which could open the door for a whole new world of shit. One ballistics examination of his 9mm could link him to several other dead whores across the US of A.

And of course, there was also the risk of pimps and thugs robbing him while he was getting serviced. Andrew knew that he'd be okay if he had the drop on someone, but it was difficult to be that secure when trying to bust a nut.

Andrew had his fun getting head and would try to get off the best he could, all before sticking his gun in their faces and getting his refund along with whatever cash they had in their purse or bra. The pimps would just have to deal with the lost revenue.

He justified his actions and attacks by telling himself continuously that he was just looking for love, or trying to fill that void left by his mother and his miserable upbringing. Making himself the victim, he found validity and virtue in his actions. One day, he thought, he would find that special someone who would fall in love, come back to him, and ask him to never leave. Until that day, everyone he talked to was as good as dead; men and women alike. They all deserved to die and he would get to decide where and when.

No longer enjoying the risks associated with meeting prostitutes in the wild, he started looking online for the women who posted ads on Craigslist. He was taken back by the ease and accessibility that the internet age had brought to the world's oldest profession.

Most of them appeared to be scammers, or the types of girls who wanted to sell their services over the phone. Andrew had no need for this. It would take some hunting, but Andrew was able find a girl each night on which to spend his time, money, and semen. He figured that this would provide a better opportunity to look for true love, feeling that there was a certain level of classiness to calling an escort and meeting in a hotel, as opposed to picking one up off the street like a stray cat.

Andrew started paying for the hotel rooms. He had reached a new apex in his life where he didn't need to live like a slob anymore. He was a professional fucker and killer and he now had the kind of money where he could live like a true titan of industry. He also believed that if he proved he had his shit together then the right woman might enter his life and stay a while; the kind who would see him as a protector. Some of the escorts looked like they had potential but all of them thus far had failed to live up to expectation.

Andrew wanted to find a woman's heart. He knew that if he waited long enough and cast his line for that special fish in the sea, he would meet the right one who knocked his socks off. She would be a victim of her time, and he would at last have a person to save.

15

"Shit," Faith murmured while getting out of her car and looking at the hotel she hoped to not see again for a while. She was supposed to be off work getting stoned with Bethany, not escaping the paramedics and police detectives analyzing her corpse. Still, Faith understood the precarious nature of her situation and accepted that she had no better options.

She opened the trunk and took out one of the trash bags that she had filled with clothes. It was one among many that held her life's possessions. Almost poetic that everything she owned fit nicely into these trash bags, each sitting inside the trunk of her busted up Cobalt. Even Faith laughed at the coincidence. She hadn't laughed aloud in a while so this was an odd but welcoming change of pace; even if it was at her own expense.

Shivering with the late night she walked toward the hotel, seeing Andrew again propping open the door from the side. He was dressed in sweatpants and a white t-shirt this time; perhaps his own way of acknowledging that this wasn't a hook-up, but rather a potential opportunity to save a damsel in distress.

Seeing Faith walk toward him with a full trash bag swung over her shoulder, Andrew could pick up that she'd hit rock bottom. He saw Faith as a woman who needed him; the one who would give him purpose, save his life, and in doing so, ultimately save her own. He smiled at her.

"It's good to see you again," he told her while holding the door open like a gentleman.

"Thanks," she said instinctively. "I've had a bad night and you're the only person I know around here who might not try to kill me or send me to jail."

Andrew laughed clumsily as though she were making a joke. He couldn't help but think about how those odds were still on the table. He had been fascinated with her story and was compelled to ask how the rest of her evening went.

"My roommate died at our apartment, and her boyfriend slash drug dealer probably wants to pin it on me..." Faith replied as cold as the night air. "I'll tell you more about it later if you want. Not right now."

Andrew didn't try to dig any further. He knew he would get the whole story soon. He took her inside and led her back to the room that he had tidied up a bit since she'd left.

"I'm glad you're back... sorry if I've said that before," Andrew reminded her.

Faith walked into the room and checked the environment again to ensure it was still safe. She looked at the camera that was still perched on the tripod. The red light was on, showing that Andrew was going to take another picture when she was ready. It made her uncomfortable but she didn't want to complain yet. Faith needed a place to stay and Andrew felt like the most logical and illogical choice. She reached in her purse for her little bag that contained her last bit of cocaine - her most valuable possession - and made a bee line back to the bedside table. Andrew stopped her before she could pour out the contents.

"You need to stop doing that shit if you're going to stay here," he stated.

Faith glared at him with the most visceral expression that she'd ever given a man. It was almost more hateful than the look she gave her parents, or Sammy, or even Ty. No one gets to fucking tell her what to do.

Andrew was at first reluctant to dictate her in this fashion. This was the closest that he ever had to a real partner and she would need to know her place. It was imperative that she learn to follow directions while also being a loving and comforting partner. In return he would give her protection.

As long as she stayed and obeyed him, she'd never have to worry again. He had it all under control.

"What's with the camera still on?" she asked, now irritable. On any other night she would have told him to go fuck himself. Being that he was letting her stay she felt the need to oblige for now and lay off the blow. At least for one night.

"I just like to record things," he replied, "does it bother you?"

"Yes, a lot," Faith replied. Things were getting worse for her, but if there was anything she could have control over it was going to be this.

Andrew was annoyed, but out of respect for his new girlfriend he turned the camera off and sat across from Faith on the opposite bed.

"You don't have to go into detail right now, but I'd like to know what you're trying to do. Is this something we need to leave town for tonight or can we stay here until morning?"

Faith was amazed that Andrew was willing to get this involved in her drama. "I think we can wait," she said, "no one except for Beth knew that I was coming here."

"Good," Andrew answered, also seeing it as a plus in case things went sour and he had to take care of her in a different way. "You can stay here as long as you agree to let me help you."

Faith was confused by what he had just said, but agreed anyway to avoid further dialogue.

She was pleased to take a hot shower. The water caressed her skin and for a moment Faith was able to forget about who and where she was. Her station in life was miserable, and despite what Andrew was saying, it wasn't likely to get better anytime soon.

"What's with this guy?" Faith questioned under her breath while running the hotel-provided shampoo through her hair.

She would have plenty of time to find out later. For now, she was just happy to be in a bathroom that wasn't covered in grime; to have a sink that wasn't buried in cheap makeup and perfumes; one that didn't have a dead hooker lying nearby.

Faith thought about the situation she had just left and compared it to the cleanliness and implied safety of Andrew's hotel room. She started to hope that maybe Andrew was alright. Outside of a few quirks he hadn't shown any signs that he would harm her, like, really harm her. Maybe this was the night that things would change and this Andrew guy would be the one to save her from this shitty life. A girl could only hope.

Andrew lied in bed in his underwear, thinking about what his remaining days could be like with Faith by his side. He was hesitant to say he was in love with her, and her pussy wasn't the best he'd had, but there was something about her that drew him in.

Maybe it was that she stayed and talked to him, or that she came back, proving that there was something about him that she liked too. Andrew was certain that if he said the right things at the right time then she would eventually fall for him as well. Out of all the other whores that he'd been with, she was special. And as long as she stayed by his side, he would do everything he could to take care of the rest.

He was nearly asleep when Faith came out of the bathroom with a towel wrapped around her body. She dug into her trash bag to find a clean change of clothes and slipped them on before joining Andrew in his bed. Even with a second queen available she felt obligated to lay down next to him. She also liked the prospect of cuddling with someone who wasn't paying to fuck her; or wouldn't try to rape her in her sleep; or wouldn't get pissed off and wake her up with a punch to the jaw.

They rested together peacefully in a spoon position. Faith tried to go to sleep but when she closed her eyes, all she could see was Bethany's cold, pale face staring up at her, the fear frozen in her dead eyes.

Andrew was unaware of her disturbance as he stared at the back of her head in serenity, smiling at the beautiful woman sharing his bed. Thoughts of their future excited him, and soon he had an erection that poked the crack of Faith's ass. Her eyes widened with annoyance at his member for interrupting her train of thought. She knew what Andrew wanted but she was in no mood to let him fuck her again.

Losing her coke, seeing her dead friend, and then driving off to escape the police was not the kind of foreplay that put Faith in the mood. Andrew didn't say anything but Faith knew that he wasn't going to let up without relief. Men are too needy for that.

Wanting to put it to rest she sat up and removed the covers from the two of them, exposing Andrew's hard cock sticking up through the slip in his boxers. He looked up at Faith, implying her to take the lead, hoping and wondering if she would. Not wanting his dick anywhere near her vagina, Faith decided to take care of the problem with her hands. She reached down and gently stroked his penis, while using her other hand to fondle his balls.

Andrew moaned and laid his head back on the pillow. While Faith continued stroking, Andrew looked at her tits and remembered his mother's breasts in the moonlight. In a move that surprised even Faith, Andrew sat up, stopping the hand job, and adjusted himself so that he could lay across her lap.

With his dick still at attention she resumed her part; surprised again when Andrew started sucking and nibbling on her nipple. It shouldn't have taken her back that Andrew had a nursing fetish, but if it got him off quickly and allowed her to get some sleep then she was open to it. His sucking became more aggressive the closer he came to orgasm, soon giving her a full painful bite the moment he ejaculated and covered Faith's hand with his cum.

He released her nipple from his mouth and re-adjusted himself off her lap and back to a normal sleeping position. As Faith wiped his semen onto the sheets, she almost felt sorry for Andrew until he said something that shook her.

"Thank you, Mommy," Andrew whispered.

Faith winced. "What the fuck is wrong with you?" she lipped silently before turning back to her side position, hoping that she could soon fall asleep.

16

The rain had stopped by the following morning, allowing for the clouds to break and the sun to come out. Andrew slid out of bed and dressed himself quietly to avoid waking Faith. She looked like an angel laying in his bed. He took a moment to gaze at the sleeping beauty and think about how lucky they were to have found each other. Smitten, he picked up his camera from the table and took a few pictures, leaving the flash off so as to not disturb her.

"What are you doing?" Faith asked, awakened by his movement and the noise from the photoshoot.

"Oh, nothing," he said calmly, placing the camera back down on the desk. "We need to check out by 11 though, so we should get some breakfast while we can."

Faith wasn't accustomed to being awake before noon. She didn't mind that morning since he had given her a place to stay. The least she could do was play nice.

As soon as they were both dressed Andrew walked to the bathroom to take a piss. Idly waiting for him to finish, Faith stood in the room and noticed that the camera was still turned on and sitting on the desk beside her. She looked toward the bathroom to make sure she was out of eyesight, then curiously picked up the camera. She shuffled through the recent photos; at first creeped out by the ones he took of her sleeping, but also impressed with how hot she looked the previous night despite being coked up and traumatized.

When she got past the photos of herself, she found a series of obscure shots of landscapes and buildings. There seemed to be no logic or skill. It was almost like he was taking pictures at random. Thumbing quickly through the gallery, she finally came across one that raised questions. It was a shirtless woman on her stomach laying on a sidewalk surrounded by liquid. Faith couldn't determine if it was water, blood, or urine. She tried to figure out how to zoom onto the photo, but-

"Put that down!" Andrew commanded, stepping out of the bathroom.

Faith looked at him and froze, "I was just looking at the pictures from last night."

She wanted to ask about the woman, but instead thumbed away from it, trying to hastily return to the more recent photos.

"Put it down right now," he ordered again.

Faith complied and set the camera back on the desk, backing away.

Andrew walked over and picked it up, observing the screen to make sure Faith hadn't seen anything she shouldn't have.

"I need you to never touch this again," Andrew said.

"Okay. Sorry," Faith said timidly. She didn't know where this assertive side of Andrew was coming from, but it started to feel like she was talking to a complete stranger.

"That's okay. You didn't know," his voice softened, "come on, let's get something to eat."

The Holiday Inn had the typical continental breakfast that's present at every mediocre hotel across America, consisting of an assortment of Danish pastries, cereal, coffee, and juice concentrates.

Faith couldn't stop fidgeting while she and Andrew sat across the table from one another silently eating their food. It had been eight hours since her last bump and she could feel herself getting antsy. While Andrew obnoxiously chewed on his Raisin Bran, Faith strategized how she could get away for a moment to get her fix. Her precious vice was stuffed in her bra so it would only take a few minutes to sneak away and scoop out a quick hit of booger sugar.

She didn't want to look suspicious though, so in the mean time she figured this would be a good opportunity to figure out what was up with the strange man who called her "mommy" last night.

"So, why are you here?" Faith asked.

Andrew looked up, still chewing on a spoonful of cereal. He swallowed and washed it down with a gulp of orange juice.

"You mean, what brings me to Richmond?" he asked.

Faith didn't nod or say anything. She was just making conversation. He could have said anything and it would have been the same to her.

Andrew responded anyhow, "I've been driving across the country for almost a year now. I'm actually from Washington state, but I've been on the East Coast for a few weeks."

Faith was mildly curious. "Where are you gonna go now?" she asked, taking a sip of her coffee.

Andrew paused for a few seconds, trying to figure out the right words to say. "Well, I guess that depends on you."

Faith scrunched her eyebrows and looked at him confused.

"I'm involved in your life now and you're involved in mine. I'll go with you wherever you need to go." Andrew tried to make himself sound more charming than weird. He could tell by Faith's body language that he had failed at that task.

Faith excused herself to search for the public restroom near the lobby. The restroom by the front desk was for employees only but it was too early in the morning for Faith to give a shit. While sitting in the stall Faith started to question if it was a good idea to stay with Andrew. He was fucking odd and he had that bizarre picture of a woman. What the hell was up with that?

She wondered if he was on the autism spectrum, or if he was a psychopath who wanted to rape and murder her on the side of the road. Anxious, she took the coke out of her bra and stuck in her finger, scooping out a nail full of powder. She brought it to her nose and snorted with the ferocity of a starving woman who had just found a loaf of bread. It felt like days since she had had her last hit, and the dopamine washed over her in an awesome way. Faith sat for a few minutes to let it travel down to her esophagus, while thinking about Andrew and the kind of man he thinks he is; and the balls he had telling her not to get high around him.

She was about to have a second dose before noticing that it would mean finishing the bag. Maybe she was wrong in her apprehension for Andrew. Maybe he wasn't that bad of a guy. He did offer her a free room in this fucked up "no one rides for free" world. Perhaps he was just a lonely man, thirsty for companionship and needing to feel a sense of dominance. She had met men like that in the past; the ones that would want to stick around after sex. Faith usually hated it when men got like that. They assumed that just because they paid to fuck her, she would be somehow required to kiss them on the mouth and act like a wife. This was the category she believed Andrew fell into. Loaded with cash, but too awkward and desperate to meet someone nice enough to suck his dick once in a while.

Faith also considered that he could potentially be the best thing that ever happened to her. Maybe he would take her to New York and she could be that actress she dreamed of being when she was a little girl. It wasn't likely, but she wasn't ready to let the dream go just yet.

After looking in the mirror to make sure there was no powdery residue on her face, Faith walked out of the employee restroom and found Andrew still sitting alone at the table.

"You feeling alright? You were gone a while," Andrew spoke without tact.

Faith found it strange that Andrew felt so comfortable around her that he would ask personal questions like that.

"I'm fine," she said.

Her answer seemed to satisfy his curiosity. "So, where do you need to go from here?" he asked.

"I don't fucking know," Faith replied, resting her forehead on her hand. "I don't think I really have anywhere to go. The cops are probably looking for me, so I think I just need to get out of here."

"Is there anyone who could help you for a little while until you got back on your feet?" Andrew asked, hoping that she would say no and be stuck relying on him forever.

Faith thought about it. "My parents, I guess. They're the only ones who know I still exist. I don't think they'd help though. They never have."

Andrew pondered the things that Faith had told him about her parents and shared her anger. He was certain that they needed to pay for what they did to her.

"I think we should go to your parents' house anyway," Andrew recommended, "they owe you for all the shit they put you through."

"That's a fucking stupid idea," Faith protested.

But Andrew was relentless. "Trust me, you'll feel better once you get everything off your chest. And afterward I'll take you wherever you want to go. I'll even take you all the way to New York."

Faith was puzzled by Andrew's sudden pressure to visit her mom and dad, but it was better than staying put and waiting. Plus, there was the slim possibility that they were different people now and they'd welcome her back into their home with open arms.

Faith watched Andrew finish packing up the room. Once he was done, she slung her trash bag over her shoulder and walked with him outside. She made a brief stop at her car to gather the rest of her luggage and necessities. No longer having a need for her own vehicle, she decided that she'd leave it and presume that the hotel management would have it towed within the week.

She didn't really care at this point. She just wanted to leave. While gathering the rest of her belongings she also checked inside her purse to make sure Andrew hadn't taken her cash. It would be just her fortune that he would try to scheme his money back after all of this. She thought it would be best to nip that in the bud right then and there.

Walking back to Andrew, she saw him staring into the window of a Honda Civic with his Jeep Cherokee running a few feet away.

"Listen," she said, "I want you to know the money you gave me last night is mine. I'm not giving it back to you."

Andrew didn't answer her. Instead, he struck a lead pipe into the driver side window of the Civic, shattering the glass. The car alarm sounded off while Andrew swiftly popped the locks and got to work inside the vehicle. In less than two minutes he had found a wallet, an MP3 player, and a cell phone charger.

In record time he ran to the driver seat of the Cherokee and shouted at Faith.

"Here's my car. Get in quickly. Hurry!"

"Holy shit! What are you doing?" she asked in panic.

"Don't worry about that right now. Just get in!"

With her heartbeat racing, Faith ran to the passenger side as instructed and slid in, slinging her trash bags to the back floorboard.

Andrew sped out of the parking lot, leaving Faith's car and the shattered Civic alone in the distance.

Faith was aroused by the thrill. Considering Andrew's quick action and their smooth getaway she figured that this was not the first time he'd broken in and ripped off someone's car. She wanted to ask him what that was all about, but there was already too much going through her head. For the moment she was alright with riding shotgun and wondering where or how the hell this story was going to end.

17

They had been on the road for a half hour when Faith's heart rate had finally steadied. This helped end her search for pursuing police cars and flashing lights.

She had been quiet through most of the trip so far, only speaking when giving Andrew directions to go east on I-64. In her mind, she was still having trouble comprehending why this man whom she met less than 24 hours ago was suddenly being so nice to her. No man had ever treated her this way, including the ones who had been her long-term customers. Outside of the stories she told him, the only thing that Andrew knew about her was that she was an escort with a tight pussy and a coke habit.

"Why are you doing this," she asked, breaking the silence.

Andrew had been driving without speaking much either. He was content with just listening to the radio.

"Doing what?" he asked.

"Helping me. Driving me up to my parent's house. Everything. Why are you doing all of this for me?"

"Because I love you," he quickly answered.

Andrew had been acting on his emotional instincts this whole time, so he was surprised that Faith hadn't picked up that all his recent actions stemmed from his feelings for her. He figured that she must have been too stressed out to see the obvious signs. Still, Faith didn't react the way he expected.

"Shit, man! We only just met last night. Whatever's going on in your head is something you need to get checked out because there's no way that you're suddenly head over heels for me. I'm a fucking hooker for God's sake! You're acting like I'm the first pussy you've had or something." Faith had to stop herself.

Seeing this as merely a lover's quarrel, Andrew resisted reacting in the same way he normally would. He was angry alright, but Faith was a different kind of person. She was a special one and Andrew wasn't ready to reach for his gun and put an end to their relationship. He believed that they would get through this hiccup and come out on the other side stronger than ever. He still needed for her to know that he was upset.

"I'm not an idiot. After everything I've done, how's it not obvious that I care about you? I'm doing everything I possibly can to make your life better. That has to mean something!" Andrew exclaimed.

"You sound like a fucking crazy person right now," Faith said sternly.

"Well, I'm not the one with a dead hooker roommate and a drug dealer looking for me," Andrew replied, coming off harsher than he wanted to be.

"Fuck you…" Faith said in response.

She wanted to tell him to stop the car and she would find her own way home. However, she was almost an hour's drive from her apartment and she couldn't go back to Richmond anyway. She was stuck for the time being having to deal with Andrew's behavior.

Andrew on the other hand was pissed. He was taken back to the times when he was a kid, being picked on at school and turned down by the girls in his class. He thought about the rejection he got from all the bitches he met throughout his young adult life. That cunt from the diner who didn't see him as boyfriend material. All those fucking hookers he came inside who would then try to leave the minute their time expired.

He didn't know how to process his anger with someone like her. She was the closest thing he'd ever had to an actual partner, which in its own way was uncanny. His life had led to this moment and this was his first chance at happiness. He wasn't going to trample over it by releasing his rage directly onto her.

Andrew's foot pressed down on the gas pedal causing the Cherokee to accelerate. His mind went into a trance, thinking about how much he wanted to hurt someone. Faith pretended not to notice. Ty used to pull the same shit when he was mad at her, and she learned a long time ago to just keep quiet when a man does irrational, juvenile stunts like this. She figured that if she ignored him long enough, he would stop and they could both a have a normal, level-headed, conversation.

Half a mile away there was a crouched man next to his Outback changing a flat tire. His wife and children waited on the shoulder of the road watching him work, unbeknownst that there was a Cherokee driven by Andrew moving toward them at 80 MPH. Andrew saw them in the distance and discovered a clever way to take out his anger without directly hurting Faith.

Drawing closer to the family, Andrew swerved to the shoulder of the road. Faith lifted her head from the window and perked up to the sound and feel of the road's divots warning her that they had driven out of their lane. The family hadn't noticed what was happening yet, but they would soon enough. Andrew wasn't certain if he wanted to kill just the man or the whole family, but his madness was thick and any resulting carnage would have left him satisfied. Andrew predicted that they'd probably hit their car as well, lose control, and flip a few times over the ditch before he and Faith both met their demise. A divine indication that neither of them were meant for this world.

They were less than 50 yards away when the family noticed that something terrible was happening. The man and his family jumped away from the road to escape the path of destruction, while Andrew was now driving fully on the shoulder prepared to send this family straight to Hell. He picked up speed as he got closer and closer.

"Jesus Christ! What the fuck are you doing!" Faith yelled.

Her interruption broke Andrew out of his homicidal daze and motivated him to snap back to reality. He turned the wheel, going over the divots again, and putting the Cherokee back in its proper lane. Looking in the sideview mirror, he could see the family crying and embracing one another, with the father looking at him from a distance, cursing, and having a similar look of hostility in his eyes.

"Sorry about that…" Andrew said collectedly.

Faith looked at him, again wondering if he really was a psychopath, and if getting in the car with him would wind up being the worst mistake of her life.

Faith hadn't taken her eyes off Andrew ever since he nearly hit that family. The look of disgust on her face had not faded either.

"You're not the man you pretend to be," she said to him.

"Perhaps not," Andrew replied, possibly the first time he'd been honest with himself in a while. "I like you though, a lot. And just like you I have nowhere to go; just a tumbleweed blowing in the wind… I guess that's why I fell for you so hard. You're just like me."

I am nothing like you, you twisted fuck, Faith thought but avoided saying. She was afraid that triggering him again would lead to another incident.

Another hour on the interstate and Faith could smell the salty air of Hampton Roads. It was the first time she'd been home in two years and she felt sick to her stomach seeing it all again. This was the place she left, intending to never return, and nothing about this afternoon was giving her comfort. Faith gave simple directions, instructing Andrew where to turn, feeling ill from seeing the houses of her old neighborhood, the boats lined up at docks along the marinas.

She saw people outside that she recognized. She wondered how their lives had been without her there despite never having talked to them. The sunshine over the neighborhood juxtaposed how Faith was feeling and she thought it would have been more suiting to come home the previous day when it was gray, cold, and rainy. At least then it would have fit the mood.

Faith felt intense apprehension as Andrew turned onto her street and she saw the house where she grew up. She held her breath while they approached the driveway. There was a different car there, a Toyota Camry, which made Faith wonder if her parents were still living in the house, or if someone else had moved in shortly after she left. Observing the trash and debris in the front yard and porch, she came to terms that this was the same old house with the same old people.

"This is it," Faith said, causing Andrew to stop in front of a white rancher with black shutters. She opened the door as soon as Andrew turned off the engine and stretched, looking up at the sky. Bitterness was hanging over the structure like a cloud.

"Do you want me to come with you?" Andrew asked.

"No, I'll go in by myself. Please wait here though, in case they don't answer."

"I won't leave you," he replied.

Faith shook off the weird response and made her way to the front door. She had trouble with each step forward and thought about turning back. Seeing that she had already come this far, she kept moving forward.

Faith didn't see him doing it, but she could hear Andrew's camera taking a picture as she got closer to the porch.

"Fuck", she whispered to herself. And with that she took a deep breath, straightened her posture, and knocked repeatedly on the door.

18

No one answered. Faith considered again calling the whole thing off and going back to Andrew to figure out a new plan. Maybe they could both agree to forget about this whole day and live like vagrants for the rest of their lives. Faith thought about the two of them living in hotels together; with him making money somehow and her fucking him as a means of staying in the picture. It would be a continuation of her shitty life, but it would be less work than what she would have to put in talking to her parents. She knocked one more time deciding that she would leave if there was no answer.

Just as Faith was about to turn around her ears perked to the sound of footsteps inside. Despite the anxiety knotting in her stomach, she was going to stay to see who opened the door. At least then she'd feel like she tried. She listened to the three locks turn and click before the door creaked open, revealing the silhouette of the woman who had given birth to her. There was a long silence between Faith and her mother while they remained standing at the doorway in astonishment, studying how much the other had aged. Jill had lost weight and was no longer trying to dye the gray out of her hair. Faith had changed from the skinny teenager who had left the house, to this sad, pale, cocaine-addicted prostitute with dry skin.

"Hey," Faith said. It was the only thing she could come up with.

Jill battled for her own words. Her eyes watered with both joy and disappointment in seeing how Faith had been taking care of herself. Faith's hair was stringy, she wore too much makeup, and she had the distorted face of someone who had been doing hard drugs for too long. Not being able to communicate with words, Jill stepped out onto the porch and embraced Faith with a hug. Even with the foul history between the two of them and the bitterness that festered, Faith was still her only child.

"Come inside," Jill said, holding the door while taking note of Andrew waiting in the driveway.

Faith also looked back to Andrew, who remained leaning on his Cherokee watching them, camera in hand. Faith then followed her estranged mother into the house.

"How've you been?" Jill asked.

If only you knew or really cared Faith thought. "Fine," she replied anyhow.

"That's good," Jill said. "Jake, come in here! You're not going to believe this!"

She looked to Faith, noticing that she appeared sick and malnourished. "Are you hungry? Can I get you anything?"

Faith shook her head as her father entered the living room with the same shock that Jill had when she opened the door. However, his reaction conveyed less delight and was more along the lines of confusion.

"Wow… I never thought I'd see you again," he said. Jake always had a way with words.

"Yeah," Faith said back. Tension developed between the three of them as they each wondered the purpose of this visit. There was obviously a lot they needed to talk about, but neither of them could figure out how to move the conversation forward.

"Where have you been all this time?" Jake asked.

"Living in Richmond," Faith replied almost robotically. "I have an apartment with a friend of mine."

Her parents didn't need to know the details.

"Are you still seeing Ty?" Jake asked.

"No," Faith answered, almost sounding defeated.

"That's good. I didn't think he-"

"He died last year," Faith interrupted.

"I'm sorry to hear," Jake said, "but what I was saying is that you're much better off without him."

Faith didn't say anything in response. She knew that if she did, she would get upset, tell them both to kill themselves, and then leave without accomplishing anything.

"We're happy to see you, sweetheart. We really are," Jill said, hoping to ease the pressure.

"Absolutely," Jake followed.

Jill attempted to keep the situation light, "I have a pot of coffee made. Why don't we talk in the kitchen?"

Both Faith and her father agreed with the plan, following Jill to the kitchen table where they used to eat together years ago. Faith eyed the liquor cabinet that she had raided numerous times as a teenager, remembering how it was always filled with enough booze to help her forget the many pitfalls of her adolescent life. While she sat down with her parents, she recalled that she hadn't had a drink in 24 hours, which felt like a new record for her. It had also been five hours since her last pinch of blow, making her think that she might be turning over a new leaf.

"So, who's the guy outside?" Jill asked, "your boyfriend?"

"No, he's someone I met the other day," Faith answered, now thinking about her unintended streak of sobriety.

"You got in a car with someone you barely know and drove across the state?" Jake asked, "do you at least know his name?"

"Jake," Jill said, "please stop."

"Does he think you're going to sleep with him? Is that why he's doing you this favor?" he continued.

"Jake!" Jill shouted, "Faith just got here. At least let her sit for a little while before you jump down her throat."

By now the anger that Faith had been harboring was on the verge of erupting out of her body. She was already regretting her trip back home. This had definitely been a mistake.

"Sorry," Jake said, "it's just a lot to not see you for two years, then have you just show up looking the way you do. To be frank, you look like you've been through the gutter."

Faith was losing patience with her father. She was taken back to the time she tried to seek help from her parents after being raped and they instead made her feel like a stupid, lying, slut.

91

Jake stared down his daughter. Faith looked like she was about to cry, but not out of shame. There was only wrath steering her ship.

"Forget it," he said, standing up from the table.

Faith finally spoke up, "I fucking hate you both."

"Then why did you come back here!?" Jake shot back.

Jill took this opportunity to chime in as well. "We worried so much about you. I can't believe you'd come back here and not say sorry for all you put us through."

"I can't believe you never apologized for being terrible parents and ruining my fucking life!" Faith shouted.

"We ruined your life?" Jake interjected, "look at you! You look like you're on dope, and God knows how many fucking diseases you have. You look like a fucking prostitute!"

"I am a fucking prostitute, asshole! All I ever wanted was for you and Mom to help me growing up and you never did nothing but make me feel like shit!"

"You're so dramatic, and you obviously haven't learned to take responsibility for anything!"

Jill started to cry. This wasn't the reunion she expected when she saw Faith on the front porch.

Faith was letting it pour out. She couldn't stop. "When Sammy raped me, you never did anything to help. You just treated me like shit and blamed me for it like it was my fault!"

"You're so full of it!" Jake shouted, slamming his hand on the table. "Is this why you're here? To dig up dirt from the past and try to make your mom and me feel bad? Listen, we're sorry we weren't Leave it to Beaver with you, but you weren't the easiest kid to raise; and you know that."

"Why was it that after I needed help, neither of you stepped in to save me? Why did you make me have to live like a whore after I turned 18?" Faith asked, tears now falling from her eyes.

"You need to take responsibility and save yourself!" Jake answered.

There was another moment of dreadful silence. Jill didn't say anything to break it this time; the same way she didn't say anything helpful back when Faith was a kid. The three remained in the kitchen knowing there wouldn't be any resolution. This was a fight that would go on for eternity if they allowed it.

Jake finally spoke up. "You coming here was a mistake. I don't know what you wanted, or why you thought you'd come back now. But, clearly coming back here was a mistake. Get the hell out of my house and never come back."

"I'm not going anywhere." Faith said sternly. In reality she wasn't sure where she would go anyway. She never thought she'd be allowed to stay at home, but she had some bits of optimism that this trip would help her gain something, and maybe even hit the reset button on their familial relationship. When her mom hugged her on the porch there was a brief moment where Faith thought she might even be able to re-establish herself in Norfolk.

None of that seemed like it was going to happen though.

In a fury that both Faith and Jill had witnessed many times in the past, Jake walked to his only daughter and grabbed her by the arm, jerking her out of the seat and onto her feet. There would surely be a bruise where he squeezed. It wasn't the first time she'd been bruised by a man and it certainly wouldn't be the last.

"I said leave," Jake commanded.

"Jake, come on. Please," Jill whined moving toward the two.

"Stop it, Jill. This ends now. She's leaving," Jake ordered, while forcefully pulling Faith out of the kitchen.

Back in the living room Faith managed to pull away from her father's grip and with all her tired strength punched him in the chest. It felt good to strike him, but it wasn't enough to diffuse the situation. Just as fast as she recoiled, he had already worked up enough inertia to raise his hand and slap her face. Perhaps he didn't intend on it, but his hit was enough to send her flying backward to the sound of her mother screaming.

"Stop it!" Jill shouted, "For God's sake, just stop it!"

Faith and her father looked at each other with the same animosity they had protected for decades. "Come on," he said solemnly, "it's time for you to go."

Faith understood that this wasn't a fight she would win. She walked with him to the door and waited for him to send her away for a second time.

As Jake opened the front door, sunlight shined into the house and in the doorway stood Andrew patiently. Faith wondered if he'd been there the whole time. What concerned her more, however, was that Andrew was no longer holding his camera by his side, but rather his trusty 9mm semi-automatic.

"Hello," Andrew said calmly, before raising the gun and putting four bullets into Jake's chest. Jill screamed, taking Andrew's attention away from the hemorrhaging man falling to the floor. He looked at Jill and fired off three bullets directed at her; two going into her chest and one hitting her in the face. Faith froze with fear, expecting that she would be next to die, but the gunshots never came for her. Andrew put the 9mm back in his waistband and stepped into the house.

"The things I do for you," he said to Faith, "come on. We have to hurry."

19

Outside, clouds had moved in from the north leading to a heavy shower that covered Faith's neighborhood. Rain pattered the roof, keeping a steady rhythm in contrast to the sporadic slap of nearby tree branches against the window panes. The change in weather correlated fantastically with the events that had just unfolded inside the Bishop residence.

Andrew had already checked Jake's pockets for his wallet. Faith idled in the living room, dumbfounded and wondering if this were all a bad dream.

"Grab some food from the kitchen and any booze you can find," Andrew directed, "I found your dad's wallet. We only have a few minutes before we'll have uninvited visitors... Did your parents have a specific place they kept their valuables?"

Faith was still in a daze.

"Come on! Either you help me or we have to leave the house now!" Andrew barked.

In a zombie-like state, Faith grazed through the house, pointing at her mom's jewelry box and her purse. Andrew swung the purse over his shoulder then went back to work loading his pockets with everything he could. Still having difficulty processing the afternoon, Faith quietly walked back into the kitchen and over to the liquor cabinet. The cabinet was well stocked like she remembered. Not having the energy to carry much, she found a bottle of vodka and a bottle of gin that she thought would fit the mood of the day quite nicely. When she returned to the living room Andrew was ready to walk out the door. Faith took one last look at her blood-soaked parents on the floor and then followed him out.

"The things I do for you," Andrew said for the second time as Faith trailed behind him, getting herself soaked in the storm.

Within five minutes of her parents hitting the ground Andrew and Faith were back in the Cherokee, now driving toward any place that wasn't a childhood neighborhood. They passed police cars driving peacefully, indicating that they hadn't been clued in about the house incident yet. Faith expected that the emergency services would jump into action as soon as one of the neighbors phoned in the gunshots, if they hadn't done so already.

"We'll need to get out of town just to be on the safe side. Maybe we can find a hotel in Chesapeake," Andrew suggested.

Faith was still thinking about having seen a total of three dead bodies in the last 24 hours. This was also the third time in 24 hours that she had to evade the cops and anyone who might be looking for her. Her life had become a spiral, giving her no control or idea of what was happening. She was unable to dictate where she was going to go, or how she was going to survive. Everything that she knew was gone and strangely, the only person still in her life was this crazy psychopath behind the wheel.

Watching the rain stop and the clouds begin to clear on their way out of Norfolk, Faith thought about what her father had said at the kitchen table moments before he died. Apart from him being an asshole that had given her a miserable childhood, Faith couldn't ignore the truth found in his logic. She hated everything that had occurred in her life thus far, but for the first time she considered all the situations where she forced herself to rely on others to save her. Jill, Jake, Ty, Bethany, Miles – neither of them were able to protect her.

For the first time in her shit existence, she acknowledged that even though the world was wretched, she would ultimately have to be the one who pulled herself out of it and perhaps, find a normal lifestyle that wasn't so pathetic. There had to be something she could do to put an end to all of this. Faith looked at Andrew while he drove and determined that she was either going to fix her life or she was going to put an end to it; because anything was better than what she was doing now.

"I'm gonna pull off the road and get some drive-through. You hungry?" Andrew asked.

Faith had had enough. "I can't believe you killed my mom and dad," she said, her sadness and anger fusing together.

"Hey, we don't know if they're really dead. And I didn't want to have to do it, but I heard y'all fighting and no one talks to my baby like that." Andrew tried to place his hand on Faith's. She jerked it away.

"Baby!? I don't know what's going through your fucking head, but I can't do this anymore. Stop the car and let me out right now. I'm getting out of here." She spoke with an assertiveness that she hoped to maintain if she was going to change her life for the better.

Andrew exploded, not understanding why Faith would think he'd stop the car in the middle of the interstate.

"What the hell is wrong with you?" he asked, "I've done so much for you these last two days. I'm risking everything and you're sitting here being a bratty bitch about it. If you're going to be my wife you need to learn some fucking respect."

"You're a fucking lunatic! Stop this fucking car!" Faith shouted.

"We're going to the hotel!" Andrew snapped back, pressing his foot harder on the gas. "We'll talk about this when you're not so emotional."

"God damn it!" Faith screamed, grabbing the wheel and shifting the Cherokee to the shoulder of the road, feeling the rumbling divots once again.

The tires hydroplaned after hitting a rain puddle that had been pooling all afternoon. In what felt like an instant, the vehicle lost its grip on the pavement. The tail end spun. Andrew tried furiously to get it back on the road, but it wasn't enough. The Cherokee quickly slid to the ditch and tree line and there was nothing either of them were going to do about it. They braced themselves, wondering if this would be the end for them. Faith closed her eyes and waited for it all to be over.

She felt like she was on a rollercoaster. The Cherokee slid into the ditch and started rolling, coupling with the deafening sound of metal crunching and glass shattering. The airbag deployed and hit Faith in the chest while fragments of the passenger window cut the skin of her face and arms. She kept her eyes shut, anticipating the final blow that would take her out, but it never came.

Once the rolling had come to halt, Faith opened her eyes and observed the wreckage. She looked down at her clothes and wiggled her extremities to see if she was bleeding or if any of her bones were broken. To her surprise, the airbag and seatbelt had performed their jobs effectively and kept her in one piece.

Unfortunately, however, the safety components of the Jeep Cherokee had kept Andrew alive as well. Faith looked over to him and watched him groan, appearing to have suffered more pain from the crash. He deserved more pain.

"Asshole," she said while jostling herself, trying to find a way out of this trap.

Seeing what may be her only opportunity, Faith unbuckled her seatbelt and fell down to the overturned roof of the vehicle. Andrew struggled to move toward her, but couldn't maneuver his bruised and bloody arms around the airbags.

All of their belongings were now on the ground, getting wet from the puddle of water seeping in from the broken windows. Grabbing one of her trash bags and the cash spilled from the console, she found the latch to the passenger door and dragged herself out.

Now standing next to the wreckage, she couldn't believe that either of them survived. This was the sign that she needed. There was a drive in the universe that was keeping her alive through all the shit she'd experienced, and that afternoon proved it. Feeling a strange sense of optimism for the future, Faith escaped into the woods and kept running until she could no longer hear Andrew shouting her name.

20

Eight days later, Faith woke up alone to the sound of a loud ambulance passing nearby. The motel she was staying at was a block away from an old folks' home, so it didn't surprise her when an emergency vehicle came through and woke up everyone trying to sleep in.

Her current residence was the rundown Atlantic Inn situated on the outskirts of Virginia Beach, far enough in the sticks that she could remain in hiding, but close enough to civilization for her to be in walking distance to a Food Lion and 7-Eleven. More importantly, it was the kind of shady motel that accepted cash, and it was in a convenient place to meet clients and maybe a new dealer if there was one in the area. Faith wasn't a fan of the motel or her current stage. She knew she'd have to move on eventually, but for now she had everything she needed - a few changes of clothes, enough money to stay in the room for two more nights, and two bottles of her parents' liquor that she took when she escaped the crash.

Faith was fearful that Andrew might still be out searching for her and prayed that he'd gotten arrested as soon as the police arrived to the wreck, ran his plates, and found all the stolen credit cards in his console.

It had been eight days since Faith saw her parents die and eight days since she found out that Andrew was a sadistic, murdering, asshole. She hadn't run into him yet, but she knew it was her luck that he'd turn up again if she wasn't careful.

Being that she had to make the choice between eating or having a roof, Faith fixed herself a breakfast of champions, consisting of protein bars and a small bottle of malt liquor shoplifted from the 7-Eleven. This plan was okay for now, but she knew it wasn't going to work in the long run. Faith needed real money, and fast. She considered putting an ad online for her services, but every time she tried, she would become washed over with anxiety that Andrew would see it and find her. It was in her better interest to keep a low profile the best way a girl in her profession could.

On one of her evening walks back from the store she saw a used condom littered on the ground, and nearby, a fellow prostitute wearing a short black skirt and fishnet stockings, smoking a Columbian rock by the outdoor stairwell. Faith didn't interact or make eye contact. Instead, she watched from the street as a man pulled his car beside her, chatted for a moment, then parked. Faith observed the newly found couple walk into the woman's motel room where she would make her money for the night.

It went against everything Faith believed in. Although after a brief debate, she told herself that this was the safest way for her to bring in cash until she got back on her feet. Her body was bruised, but her tits still looked good and her pussy could still get wet, so she had everything she needed to get back to the office.

Faith went back into her room to put on something skankier than the hoodie-sweatpants combo she had on, then walked out into the chilly night, shivering now that she was wearing substantially less clothing. She scanned the parking lot for police, but didn't see any around which allowed her to officially open back up for business.

While she scanned the parking lot, she fumed over how much this whole circumstance royally pissed her off. She and Bethany had taken a stance long ago that neither of them would be the streetwalking type. Taking this job was a sign that she had truly hit the bottom. She wasn't a professional call-girl anymore. Now she was just a common street hooker. Outside of the paranoia that she would get hurt, she was now the type of escort who could easily find

100

herself catching a disease or getting robbed, raped, and murdered. She had to keep telling herself that this was only a temporary move and let that be her mantra as she eyed the Honda Civic slowly driving by.

The car stopped beside her and the windows came down. The man driving was overweight and greasy; nothing that she wasn't familiar with by now.

"Hi… are you, um… would you like to go on a date?" he asked nervously.

"Maybe. $200 and I'm all yours," Faith replied.

"Um, all's I got is $150."

In the before time, Faith would have told him to walk his fat ass into traffic, but she was dying to bring in some money and couldn't afford to be picky.

"That'll work this once. Let me in," she ordered.

If she wasn't getting paid her normal rate then she wasn't going to play submissive either. This was business. Faith walked to the other side of the car and the man opened the door for her from the inside.

"You're so beautiful… My name's Phillip by the way. What's yours?"

"The money?" Faith asked impatiently.

"Oh, right," Philip struggled to reach into his pocket for his wallet. Once successful, he happily pulled out the cash.

"Jessica," she replied, putting the money in her bra, "let's go somewhere dark."

"Don't you have a room here?" Phillip asked.

"No. Let's just find a place where we can get some privacy," Faith answered. One of her golden rules was also to never let the clients know where she lived.

They drove a couple miles before turning into the darkened lot at an office park.

"Is here okay?" Philip asked, like a child asking his mother if his room was clean.

"This'll be fine," Faith answered distantly.

101

Philip smiled, thinking that he had done something good, although he was still visibly anxious. "Okay, good. Sorry, I'm so nervous. This is my first time."

Faith tensed up having heard this line before. She was afraid; not because she thought this guy was going to be like Andrew, but because his words reminded her of the nice, boring man that she met that night and how he turned crazy within a few hours.

Overall, she just wished that men would stop saying that stupid line. It's not like she was going to be charmed to be popping their hooker cherry.

By the looks of this guy, she might very well be taking his cherry in general. His neckbeard was unkempt, and the hair on his balding scalp slicked back to a ponytail. It was fitting that he also wore glasses and had bad teeth. Philip put the car in park, unfastened his seatbelt, and looked at Faith, hoping that she would tell him what to do.

Faith reached over the console and unbuttoned his pizza-stained khakis. Men liked it when she took charge and helped them with these opening acts. It made them think that she was really interested in having sex with them.

After undoing his zipper, she reached into his boxers and pulled out his cock. She wanted it to be hard enough to fuck already, but he was still nervous about doing all of this in public. He probably had some semblance of a future planned for himself and didn't want a solicitation charge to appear on his record if they got caught. Faith on the other hand had nothing to lose.

With Philip's cock not being ready she'd have to take care of it herself. Just like she did before with Miles, Faith looked at his wilted member, took a deep breath and leaned over, immediately catching the smell of his unwashed taint. Having her face in close proximity to a swampy groin was something she had experienced many times, but she could never get used to it.

Trying to put her mind somewhere else, she closed her eyes and opened her mouth, guiding his penis in with her hand. She tasted the residue of urine while feeling his blood flow increase each time she raised her head. He was uncircumcised and hadn't cleaned his folds properly, causing the flavor of bacteria to cover her tastebuds. Philip moaned in pleasure and made grunting noises while she sloshed saliva around his cock and slurped it with her tongue. She knew that if she sucked too much he would release his loudest grunt to preface the disgusting string of cum that would shoot in her mouth. Her oral skills had perfected since she was in high school and soon enough Philip was stiff enough to ride.

"Do you have a condom?" Faith asked.

"Yeah! Hold on," Philip said, reaching into his wallet again for an old Trojan. He held up the condom like he had just found a gold coin and smiled at Faith.

After securing it, she commanded him to drop his seat completely back. Once there was enough room between his body and the steering wheel, she positioned herself on top of him. Guiding his cock with her hand, she lowered herself and bucked while he placed his hands on her hips. Without lubing her pussy beforehand, she felt a stab of discomfort but chose not to complain. Being that she might be the only woman he'd ever fuck, she wanted give him decent customer service. It was the least she could do.

With his dick inside her, Faith started to feel nervous again, thinking that Andrew could find them together. He would probably shoot Phillip dead on the spot and then keep her as a hostage if he didn't kill her right there also. She tried to keep telling herself that he was gone and that the odds of him finding her were next to impossible. The paranoia was strong though, and she couldn't shake it no matter how hard she tried. This is what was going through her head when Philip tightened his grip on her thighs and his body started to convulse. A loud grunt followed with the wave of semen expelling from his urethra.

"Thank you," he said, short of breath.

Faith slid off of him and moved back to the passenger seat.

"Uh oh," Philip spoke again like a child.

"What?" Faith asked, staring as he looked downward at the torn condom wrapped around his dick.

In that moment Faith began to notice the sticky substance still inside her. It was a feeling that reminded her of the squirts of lube that she would insert before meeting her clients. Except this time, it wasn't Astroglide, but the active sperm of this sloppy fat ass.

"I'm so sorry!" He cried.

Faith stuck her fingers in her pussy to gauge the amount that he had put in her. She found some Wendy's napkins on the floor that she used to scoop the majority out. The only men she ever let cum inside her were Ty and Miles, and she was amazed and disgusted that fatty Philip had now become the third.

While thinking about how much she didn't want to deal with this, her and Philip were both illuminated by two oncoming headlights. Faith's first thought was that Andrew had somehow found her, but these fears subsided when she recognized that the headlights belonged to a vehicle owned by the Virginia Beach Police Department.

"Oh, shit! Fuck!" Philip panicked, seeing the car turn on its flashing blue lights.

Scared shitless, he immediately zipped up his pants and fastened his belt while instructing Faith to pull up her underwear. When the car stopped, Faith saw there was only one officer present.

Unwilling to be arrested with Philip of all people, she took this opportunity to continue her new hobby of evading the police.

As soon as her underwear was back up covering her ass, Faith opened the passenger door and ran into the woods under the cover of darkness. The cop shined his spotlight and shouted at her through the intercom, but Faith kept running. She looked back at the cop exiting his vehicle and walking toward Phillip, who sat in the driver seat covering his face with his hands. Faith felt a minuscule twinge of guilt leaving Philip there, but at the end of the day, her concern for a strange man's well-being was slim. They were only dicks with wallets and she was only their whore. There was no reason to make it any more complicated than that. Her new mission in life was to save herself, and that's exactly what she was going to do.

21

Andrew sat by the counter at The Silver Diner, drinking his coffee and looking at the overcooked steak remaining on his plate. This was supposedly the best diner in Virginia Beach, but the food was mediocre and the waitresses were all past their ripened prime. He'd normally be able to picture anyone naked, but despite these waitresses all being the same age as his late mother, their gritty smoker coughs were quite the turnoff.

He was disappointed with the steak and eggs he had just consumed and felt the rumble in his stomach, indicating that it disagreed with him as well. Rubbing his knife across the plate he thought about Faith and his only reason for still being in this part of the country. On a normal day, Andrew would have already been in another state, hunting for his next source of income and another opportunity to get off. However, Faith was the one that got away, and he couldn't stop obsessing over the bitch.

Andrew firmly believed that Faith was the love of his life; but on the flip side of that coin, she was another worthless whore who needed to be punished. He didn't think she'd ever go back to Norfolk. Despite her not having a car, she had swiped $270 from his totaled Cherokee, so she could have easily found her way back to Richmond if she tried. Based on the way she talked about the city though, and knowing how fucked she'd be if she returned, he put his money on her still being nearby.

Andrew looked outside at his rental Toyota Camry he was now driving and would undoubtedly never return. He didn't believe his luck when the cops showed up to the accident.

After crawling out of the wreckage he hastily attempted to conceal everything; successfully offloading Faith's remaining trash bag luggage, as well as any incriminating evidence. When the police finally arrived to the scene, he gave them his license and told the same story he had been telling since he started this voyage across state lines. He was a professional photographer and writer on business. This was his mother's car that she gave him just before she died. And somehow, they always bought it.

They even ran the plates to confirm his story, and again, Andrew was surprised they didn't show up on any reports. After impounding the wrecked Cherokee, they suggested taking him in for medical care, but Andrew thought it best to politely decline their offer. The "accident" left him with a concussion, but he managed to crawl out of the overturned vehicle feeling more alive than ever. It was definitely a miracle if he ever saw one. Now he hoped that he could use some of that miracle magic to find the fucking cunt that he'd so willingly given his heart to.

Andrew pulled out his notebook and looked again at the list of places he suspected she could be. He had already checked out several bars and sketchy regions in Virginia Beach, Chesapeake, and even Norfolk, scouting out drug dealers and thugs who he thought could have sold Faith her latest batch of coke. He presumed with her habits that she'd be frequenting these locations, but he was unable to uncover any new leads. Instead, he was faced with objections and ridicule as he portrayed the image of a tired man searching for his former lover.

He crossed out the bars on the Virginia Beach strip, as well as the poor areas and ghettos in the area that were typically inhabited by local escorts. He had no luck in his search thus far and his patience was waning.

Andrew wondered if he should simply give up on his endeavor and come to terms with Faith being the flame that burned out. It was a difficult pill for him to swallow, and it was entirely her fault. He was the supreme gentleman to her and was willing to put it all on the line, all while she was too obtuse to see the big picture. They could have had a beautiful life together; maybe in New York like she had dreamed. He could have been the white knight who saved her from her terrible trajectory. If only she understood that things could be better.

Taking another sip of coffee, his thought pattern went dark. Andrew started to consider that perhaps the reason she didn't stay with him was because she was wicked like all the others. Maybe it was he that made the error in thinking she was different. Perhaps she was just like all those sluts in high school and college who rejected him, and laughed at him, and made him feel like he was a piece of shit. She was going to pay for this. Everyone was going to pay for this. Every stupid motherfucker in the world was going to one day feel his wrath and see him as the god that he was.

Yet, there was still a part of his heart that still felt soft for Faith. She was clearly troubled and in need of help. She didn't quite see it, but Andrew was sure she could be taught. Hopefully she hadn't already reverted to her old ways, doing hard drugs and whoring herself out to strangers. The fear crossed his mind that she would find another guy who would step in, claim to be the hero, and then hurt her worse than she'd already been. Andrew was determined to be the one that saved her from the world. There was a reason that he found her specifically online, that her ad popped out to him amongst all the others. He had first assumed she would be just another fuck, but her story persuaded him that she was special; a woman who could help him out as much as he could help her. In truth, he knew he was searching for a savior himself.

Looking over his notepad and thinking about the places that she would be, the idea struck him that she might have found a job at a local strip joint since that's what she was doing when she lived in Richmond. As beautiful as she was, she'd have no problem finding one nearby that would accept the honor of having her dance on stage. The more he convinced himself that this was probably the case the angrier he became at the thought of other slobs putting their hands on his woman. He knew that she hated it and was longing for him to find her and take her out of that world. He would just need to find her, somehow.

Over the next two nights he visited strip clubs all over Hampton Roads. He tried to avoid interacting with anyone at these venues who wouldn't give him his much-needed intel. Even when a girl sat on his lap and attempted to con him into a lap dance, he maintained his stoic demeanor and simply asked if they knew of Faith, or Chloe, and asked if she had been seen working there. The awkwardness would hang thick between he and the woman trying to take his money; but he didn't let that hinder him. He could just as easily bring his gun into that club and shoot everyone if it would bring him any closer to his love. His search and obsession allowed these assholes to live for another day.

The final strip club in Hampton Roads was Mermaid's in Virginia Beach, which was close enough to the coast to be populated and have a nearby grocery store, but far enough to where a girl could hide if she needed to. He decided this would be his last stop and attempt at finding her. If this ended up being another dead end then he would give up on his quest and drive somewhere else to find sex, money, and blood. Maybe New York.

Andrew pulled his rental car into the parking lot and was forced by the congestion to park further from the door than he would have preferred. The house was packed and full of assholes flaunting their money. The men smoking cigars outside near the entrance reminded him of all the douchebags that he knew growing up. All too cool for school and able to pick up any woman they wanted. Even though none of them were looking at him or acknowledging his arrival, he felt their judgement and inflated egos from a distance.

He walked into the club, immediately being greeted by a burly black man wearing a yellow security shirt and carrying a metal detecting wand. The guard scanned him just like he had all the others, making Andrew think of the 9mm that was packed nicely in his glove box. After passing security he paid his $20 to the door girl and walked in, annoyed that he had to pay the entry fee just to search for Faith. She would certainly owe him big after all this trouble. That much was for sure.

He observed the room. There were two stages on opposite sides with a girl on each, wearing nothing but a thong and pasties that matched their skin tone. He walked around briefly, observing the bartenders and searching to see if Faith was talking to any of the guys seated throughout the club. Unable to locate her, he found a seat far from the stage in the corner and sat down with a morose expression on his face. He thought the other strippers would take it as a sign that he wanted to be left alone.

His gimmick only lasted for so long. While watching the entrance of the VIP room for several songs, a sexy blonde one wearing a cowboy hat walked straight to his table and sat down next to him.

"Hey honey, I'm Dallas. How are you?" the stripper asked.

"Fine," Andrew responded.

Dallas quickly took the hint that she wasn't welcome, but assumed he might just be having a bad day, and if she cheered him up the dollar bills would spill from his wallet.

"I haven't seen you around here before," Dallas continued, stating the obvious for the sake of small talk.

"First time," Andrew clapped back.

"What made you decide to stop by?" she asked.

"Looking for someone," Andrew replied.

"Oh! Maybe I can help you. Who are you looking for?"

Andrew's eyes lit up. "Faith, er... I think she goes by Chloe when she's working. Have you seen her?"

"I think I heard about her trying to get a job here earlier in the week. They didn't take her though. I remember hearing Jeff say she looked like she would bring trouble."

This was the first clue that Andrew had received in days.

"Do you know anything else about her? Did she say where she was staying?"

"I don't think so. I didn't talk to her," Dallas replied. By this point she didn't see Andrew as a regular guy looking for his favorite dancer. She saw him as the abusive boyfriend type who was out looking to hurt someone. She didn't know anything about who he was talking about, but from this interaction alone Dallas could tell that Faith, or Chloe, needed to stay far away from this man.

"Who should I talk to then?" Andrew asked forcefully.

"I don't know," Dallas replied, getting up from the chair.

"Wait!" Andrew shouted, standing up and grabbing her wrist. "I need to find Faith. I'm not fucking around!"

Dallas threw her hand back to get away. "Don't fucking touch me!" she shouted.

Andrew had heard this line before. Dallas tried walking away and Andrew continued his pursuit. He was so close and he wasn't about to lose ground.

"Rick, get this fucking creep out of here!" Dallas called to the front door. The large black security guard at the door wasted no time approaching him.

"Fuck you," Andrew said as the guard grabbed him by the arm and forced him to the exit. Andrew tried to struggle but already knew he wouldn't win this fight. The other patrons and strippers stared at him, some laughing, while Andrew was forced to the door and pushed outside.

He lost his balance on the way and tripped onto the sidewalk, skinning his elbows. The assholes who had been standing outside welcomed him with laughter. Andrew was taken back to his youth and the embarrassment that he faced at the hands of everyone. He was reminded that the world was always against him, that no matter how old he got, or how successful he was, he would always be the kid who was picked on and never appreciated.

He had pent up this hostility his entire life, relieved only by his ability to hurt some of them individually. But things were different now. Something inside him snapped and it was now time to stop being a pussy and do what needed to be done. He accepted that he might die in the process if he wasn't careful, but tonight he was going to take the final step and put an end to all the motherfuckers who had wronged him.

Andrew choked back his tears and got up off the ground, limping as he walked to his car. He tuned out all the noise around him and became focused on the task at hand. There was a 9mm in his glovebox, along with 54 rounds that were anxious to see some action. The day of reckoning had finally come.

22

Faith gave her client a forced hug before stepping out of his Prius, still feeling dizzy and sick to her stomach. She tried her best to not let it show and regretted not taking the day off.

"Call me again soon," she said, before closing the passenger door.

She looked around the parking lot to make sure there weren't any law enforcement around hunting for prostitutes and scoundrels. With the coast clear she walked herself across the street toward the motel, without turning back to get a last look at the guy she had just fucked. There wasn't any need for goodbye kisses.

Faith closed the door behind her and put the new cash in the dresser. There was now enough money for another night under a roof. She was thankful that the front desk either hadn't yet grown suspicious of her occupation, or didn't care enough to bother her. Faith wasn't the first escort to live in their motel and she definitely wasn't the only one either.

Not wanting to keep an online presence, or venture out too far, she found her niche standing around the corner a block from the motel, or across the street to snatch up the truckers who were coming in to refuel. She liked that this gave her enough exposure to lure in the men who couldn't pass up a chance to hook up, but it was obscure enough that she could bee line back to her room if she saw a cop, or Andrew.

Women in her profession need to be able to adapt to the environment, and Faith was making the best of her situation. She had become more comfortable with doing car dates and knew she'd only have to keep it up until she had enough saved up for bigger and better things.

She would sometimes find a man with coke or pills, and for that she'd give them a premium service, usually letting them play with her ass and slip their finger in while they pounded her.

Unfortunately, these types of customers were few and far between. Not being able to find an actual dealer nearby, her stay at the Atlantic Inn was turning into an unwilling rehab clinic. She had the feeling her tolerance was also waning, and worried that she'd overdose the next time she had a full stash.

Knowing herself, she'd likely go crazy and snort the whole bag in one sitting, accidentally killing herself like Bethany. One of Faith's biggest fears still was being found like that; all bloated and blue, eyes rolled back, white foam spilling out of her mouth. It was not the look she was going for.

Seeing everyone around her die made Faith wonder if her turn would be coming up soon; or if death would be an escape that she should welcome.

She was suffering from withdrawals. The men that had their own stash would give her a pill or a line; providing a small sample taste of the old times, but it was never enough. It was nothing like the party she once knew.

With everything that had occurred, especially in past two weeks, Faith started to think that she could potentially save herself after all. She was starting to believe that she had some resemblance of control over what would happen next. She also imagined what she would do if she saw Andrew again; how he would try to hurt her, how she would try to evade him without getting shot, how she would muster the strength to fight back. The fear that he was always around was something that crossed her mind at least twice each day. Faith needed to stay sharp and calm herself, recalling that it would be a small chance in Hell that they would ever cross paths again. There was always the possibility though. She could feel it on the horizon.

23

Andrew's 9mm had a full 12-round magazine loaded into the grip. The other three magazines were stuffed in his cargo pockets. In just a few moments he was going to create the biggest art piece of his life, splattering blood and brain on the floors and sending several souls straight to St. Peter. He emptied his pockets of everything except for what he would need for the mission. He didn't want anything to weigh him down, and if he were captured or killed, which was quite possible now that he thought of it, he didn't want to be easily identified. Andrew was to be a nameless man who had taken too much bullshit in his life and was finally going to get his vengeance.

He had considered writing a letter, or manifesto as he'd call it, blaming everyone who picked on him while growing up, his dad for leaving his mom to rot, and the women that he once tried to love. They all conspired together to create the monster that he had become.

"I arrive on a pale horse. My name is Death. And Hell follows with me," Andrew mumbled to himself, trying to feel deep and sophisticated through this whole ordeal.

He crossed the parking lot with purpose, hearing the smokers outside laugh at him again as he returned to the club. While Andrew moved in closer, they started moving as well, intent on letting the security guard know that the jackass had returned for more. Andrew didn't let this deter him. He had steel in his right pocket, and in his left, enough ammunition to end nearly everyone in the building.

The security guard walked out with the guys, looking dead at Andrew.

"You'd better get the fuck back in your car right now," he said, flexing his pectoral muscles. The jerks who ratted him out stood by watching, presuming that he was about to get his ass kicked again.

Instead of speaking, Andrew replied by drawing his gun and pointing it directly at the guard who immediately abandoned his machismo.

"Holy shit!" yelled one of the bystanders as they scattered like fleas screaming "he's got a gun!" The music blasting from the club's speakers drowned out the shouting and commotion outside. The naked strippers and the rich pricks in the building were oblivious to the drama that was about to take place.

"Woah man, take it easy" the guard said, knowing that Andrew had the drop on him. He held his arms out implying that he understood his position, and for a brief second Andrew felt sympathy; remembering that father from a while ago just trying to protect his family.

The brief hesitation subsided when Andrew remembered the humiliation of being thrown out like one of Faith's trash bags. Andrew kept his gun trained on the guard, allowing his heart to fill with hate. Then, noticing tears building up in his eyes he pulled the trigger, sending a bullet into the center of the guard's forehead and spraying a mist of blood behind him.

The dead guard dropped onto the asphalt. Andrew didn't have time to observe his art. He was sure that the bark of the shot alerted everyone that shit was hitting the fan, so he would need to act fast if he was going to increase his body count on this escapade.

He walked through the front door, seeing the back of the door girl as she tried to escape into the club. She was taken out with a quick bullet to the back that no doubt pierced her lungs. Andrew then continued inside, stopping by the tip jar to take out a 20-dollar bill. He was square with the house again. Andrew laughed about this for a moment, then proceeded into the main area to get back to his mission, indifferently walking past the dying cunt lying on the floor.

The crowd inside the club had clearly figured out what was happening and hid behind chairs, under tables, behind the bar, inside the VIP room, and some of the girls even escaped to the dressing room for their illusion of safety. Andrew made a mental note to pay them a visit after he took care of some business by the stage.

"Everybody up!" Andrew shouted, taunting his victims. Killing the security guard outside broke the seal and he was now having a ball indiscriminately shooting people at random. He identified the four individuals by the stage from earlier and dispatched them with a series of shots as they knelt under their tables. The fourth person by the stage attempted to crawl away like an idiot, but this only caught Andrew's attention, causing him to send two more bullets his way, one striking his shoulder and the other in his neck.

He fired a series of shots into the bar, thinking that it would hit the people hunched behind the counter. Though, he couldn't be certain that those shots had been effective. Unsatisfied with his assumption he walked up and looked over at the scared bartender hunkered down with Dallas.

"Jack and Coke, please!" he said before firing a single shot into the bartender's chest and another into Dallas' head.

The room was now mostly silent except for the sounds of cries and whispered prayers. Andrew walked around the vicinity, picking tables at random and killing the asshole hiding underneath until he eventually became bored with the activity.

Wanting to have more fun with the whores in the building, Andrew made his way toward the VIP room and found no one. He vaguely remembered people running in there, so he searched around before finding a man and stripper hunched down in the corner. They both cried as he approached and begged for their lives. Neither of them wanted to make eye contact.

"It's okay. I'm not going to hurt you," Andrew said gently with the gun still in his grip, "look at me!"

It went against their instincts but they were able to face their fears and lock eyes with their assailant.

"See, it's not so hard," Andrew said and then shot them both in the head.

Andrew loaded the final magazine, now down to only 12 rounds, so he would have to make them count. He walked back to stage area and observed the bloodshed and the dying bodies on the ground. Not seeing any more opportunities in the open, he moved on to the doorway by the stage that led to the dressing room.

As soon as Andrew stepped inside, he was greeted with a spray of mace and a chair to the side of his head. The spray burned his eyes, while the bitch with the chair continuously tried to knock him out. The other three strippers cowered in the corner with piss streaming down their legs. His left eye had taken the extent of the mace, but he could still see with his right, which he used to fight through the pain. Andrew raised his gun and shot twice at the woman with the chair who was seemingly winning the award for "bravest slut of the year". Her prize was that the bullets went right into her skull, giving her a quick painless death. He then looked at the one who maced him and shot her in the lower gut. He had read online that gunshot wounds in the lower abdomen were almost always fatal, and they tended to hurt more than shots in other regions.

The three girls in the corner were nameless and reminded him of the ones that he'd known in the past. Nothing special about them, nothing evil, they were just the types that would have inexcusably hurt him if given the chance. He killed the three of them without giving any thought to it.

Shooting everyone inside the club had given Andrew the cathartic rush that he needed. He felt like a new man, having scratched the itch that had existed for as long as he could remember. The police sirens that he heard in the distance were his cue that the game was over. He had done what he'd come to do and felt comfort in knowing that the whole night had been a success.

Andrew exited the building, studying the parking lot that now had fewer cars, and listening to the sirens get closer and closer. Sensing that time was short he ran to his car and made his best effort to drive away inconspicuously. Travelling down the road, he passed more patrol cars than he'd ever seen in his life. It seemed that with every round fired, another cop was activated and sent to congregate around the massacre. He knew that if he was stopped, the police would notice the blood on him, track his DNA, and link the gun to all of the killings, so he would need to keep a low profile and somehow get far away from Virginia Beach if he planned to make it out alive.

He assumed that one of the survivors that fled would soon give a report to the police, telling them all about the murderous shooter driving a white Camry. He'd been lucky thus far, but he had an inkling that his luck was about to run out. Needing to ditch the car, Andrew scratched up a plan to stick up someone, then have them give him a lift out of the city. He could shoot them afterward if he felt the need. He found that he did enjoy killing. It had become his thing.

And once out of town, he could start fresh and perhaps find a new girlfriend who would take the place of Faith. Anything was possible.

He pulled into the parking lot of a rundown motel that was far enough from the city to not attract any attention, but close enough where he could observe the action nearby. As he sat in his car re-living everything that just took place, the moon shined a light on the motel and he saw something that he didn't think possible. It was as though God had shined grace on him, thanking him for purging the wicked from the Earth.

Andrew couldn't believe his luck. He couldn't wait to talk to her.

24

Faith continued her path to the motel room. She hadn't noticed her visitor in the parking lot. Had she noticed, she could have run into her room as quickly as possible and phoned the police. She didn't necessarily want to get the cops involved in her life, but Andrew had taken things to that point. She listened to all the sirens and commotion going off in the distance and knew there were more police in the area than usual. That was the reason she decided to return to the motel in the first place. Well, that and her ever present urge to vomit. She had been dealing with some serious nausea lately and she hated that it was starting to affect her work.

She reached in her purse for her room key, not noticing that her biggest fan was approaching from behind with his warm 9mm in hand. Andrew only had three bullets left, but that was enough for him to have power.

"I've been looking for you," Andrew said, startling her.

"Shit. Fuck," Faith said under her breath, trying to decide which direction to run.

Andrew pointed his gun directly at her, implying that he wasn't intending to let her get far.

He spoke calmly, "Faith, we need to talk. And don't you dare scream. If you do, I'll have to end you, and I don't want to do that."

Faith wanted to escape but was too terrified to do anything but comply.

"Okay…" she said, finally able to find her key and open her room.

The two of them stepped inside. Andrew looked around the same way that Faith did on the night they met. The difference now was that he wasn't looking for a sting or a weapon, but for any interloper who might get in the way of their little make up session.

"Have you been looking for me this whole time? How'd you get away from the wreck?" Faith asked.

"Shut the fuck up. I'm going to be the one asking the questions here," Andrew said, still looking around the room and then finally to her, "First off, why did you run from me in the first place?"

"Because you were being fucking crazy," Faith answered, kicking herself for being so direct with a man who could blow her brains out that instant.

Andrew took a deep breath. "You're still blind. I was hoping that our time apart would give you time to reflect on what we have, but I'm starting to think that you'll never see things that way."

He hoped that her seeing him would make her remember all the things he did for her; but he knew now that it was a false hope. She was just like all of the other girls. It broke his heart, but he knew what had to be done. Tears in his eyes, he raised his gun again toward Faith.

"I love you," he said, choking on his words.

Faith panicked. "Wait! Baby, I'm sorry! Let's talk about this!" she screamed.

Her survival instincts and her experience made her aware of what men wanted to hear. She didn't like entertaining the idea that she desired him. It was the only option she could think of that could keep her from being shot. Andrew kept his aim on her, but refrained from pulling the trigger. For Faith, this meant that there was still a chance that she could make it out alive.

She continued, "I've just been so confused and hurt that I pushed you away. I do love you, but I'm too damaged to be loved back..."

It was partly true. She was hoping the sympathy trip would work and Andrew would stop pointing the gun at her.

"Why didn't you just tell me that instead of running off?" he asked, lowering it to his side.

"I was just scared. My mom and dad were dead. Everyone was dead. I wasn't thinking straight," she explained, not knowing that a hell of a lot more people were now dead after his massacre at Mermaid's.

Andrew was still feeling the high from executing all those people that he displayed a rare sign of empathy. "I know your life has been a struggle, but you don't have to worry anymore. I can take care of you. You just have to trust me."

"I trust you," Faith said.

Andrew looked outside the motel and listened to the police and ambulance sirens in the distance. He knew it wouldn't be long before they caught up to him.

"We have to go," Andrew said.

"Right now?" Faith asked, "I thought we could stay here. I have another night."

Faith doubted that he'd go for that, but she couldn't pass up a chance to kill him in his sleep.

Andrew wasn't having it, "We don't have time for that. Leave your shit here and get in the car. We have to leave town right fucking now. I'll explain later."

He grabbed Faith by the arm and pulled her outside, looking around to see if anyone was watching.

Faith looked at the motel as they sped out of the parking lot. She finally had a place where she felt somewhat comfortable, and as usual, she had to see it fade into the distance. With all of her possessions left behind she questioned her ability to get through the next chapter, and wondered what the hell was going to come next.

25

They drove an hour west, back toward Richmond. Faith didn't know if Andrew was taking her back to the city, or leaving the state, and she didn't want to ask.

Instead, they sat in the car and listened to the radio with a tidal wave of thoughts rushing through their heads. The temperature was warmer than usual for late February, though Faith still felt cold and numb inside.

Faith wondered again how she was going to get through this; how she was going to save herself. She made a promise that if she managed to escape again, she would make something of her life and allow herself to know peace. She was going to rise above the coke whore she had become and truly make a difference.

Her confidence that she could be better rose at the same rate as the fear that her life would be coming to an end soon. She was sitting with a man who had killed before and would happily kill again. He was a murderer, and for some reason he treated her like a person she wasn't. Faith didn't know how long she could keep this façade going.

Andrew kept the pace with traffic, not wanting to draw attention. For all he knew, every state trooper in Virginia was out looking for him. Beneath his calm exterior he too was afraid that he wouldn't get away with it this time; that his last spree of passion would cost him everything that he'd worked so hard for.

Then it hit him like a kick in the nuts. Faith was as much a liability as much as she was a lover. In his heart and mind, he knew that she didn't really love him, and that his idea of her only existed in his head. Andrew's chest burned as he came to terms with Faith being a liar who only wanted to get away from him. *Why would she say it then,* he thought, and his question was quickly snuffed out with the realization that anyone would say anything when their life was on the line. It was difficult to ignore his feeling of betrayal each time he looked at her. He had spent so long telling himself that she was the one for him that he was blinded to the fact that she was just like the others. He decided that he was going to kill her, but not before getting closure.

Andrew took the next exit, leaving Faith even more confused as to what was going on. Not even Andrew knew where they were going. He was determined to find a place isolated enough where he could finish her off and move on. They were near Colonial Williamsburg, which normally would be a populated tourist attraction, but at this hour it provided a dark and quiet hamlet where the two of them could find some needed privacy. He pulled into a spot near the old Governor's Palace and turned off the headlights.

"What are we doing?" Faith asked, looking to Andrew, who was just sitting and staring forward, "Andrew?"

"This isn't going to work," he answered cryptically.

"What's not going to work?" Faith was now more confused.

"Us. It's not going to work" Andrew replied, "get out of the car."

Faith didn't move. She didn't like where this was going. Losing patience, Andrew got out and walked to Faith's side, pulling her out and throwing her onto the ground. Faith fell to her knees, fear filling her eyes while the acidic taste of vomit entered her mouth.

Andrew looked down at her, the gun still ready at his waist. A battle was going on in his brain between the love and hate that he felt for her.

Faith laid on the ground looking at him, afraid to get back up. Andrew unfastened his belt. He figured that fucking her for the last time would be a good way for each of them to say goodbye before they parted ways. With Faith still seated on the ground he dropped to his knees and pushed his way between her legs.

In that moment Faith decided that she wasn't going to let this man have his way with her. Ever since she started having sex for money, she hadn't been in a position to turn down a dick, but this time it wasn't business. Andrew was fulfilling his lust and would likely hurt her again and again if she let him. She pushed him back and squeezed her legs together, making an attempt to stand up.

The gun was down at his ankles, so if there was any chance for her to escape, this was it. Andrew was too powerful though, pulling her knees and making her fall back down. The struggle lasted a few seconds before he grabbed Faith from behind and collapsed her under his weight. He held onto her arm and twisted it behind her back, ready to snap it if she attempted to escape again.

With his stiff erection now pressed against her, he boldly assumed that fucking her pussy could run the risk of her feeling a sense of pleasure. Not wanting her to enjoy any second of this, he lined his cock with her anus and forcefully drove himself in. Faith screamed with the sore and sharp pain of Andrew's cock forcing her sphincter to expand. He proceeded to thrust into her repeatedly, the dry friction creating an Indian burn inside her rectum. The first time Faith was raped she laid there and hoped that it would end, but this time the pain would not let her go anywhere else in her head. She felt like this was going to kill her, and if it didn't Andrew would finish the job with a bullet. Faith always knew she would die in some sordid fashion, but never dreamed it would be like this. Not by this guy.

Andrew pulled his dick out of her ass and rolled her on her back, standing above her. He bent down and pulled her up by her hair to a seated position. Faith saw his penis directly in front of her face, covered in her blood and feces, developing a clear idea of what was coming next. Andrew pushed his cock to her mouth, parting her lips and jaw and forcing her to taste the bitterness while he raped her throat. She coughed, choking on him while he refused to give her any relief. Her gag reflex had been eliminated over the years to Andrew's pleasure as the pressure built in his balls and he knew that he was about to cum.

"I bet this is reminding you of Sammy," he said to her.

It did in fact remind her of Sammy, but only in that she hated him in the same way. Sammy was the catalyst that started her on this life and now it seemed that her life was going to end the same way. The anger and disappointment festered inside while Andrew continued to ravish her.

Faith knew that no one was going to save her from this either. If she was going to get out of this Hell then she was going to have to save herself. Not giving it another thought, Faith sunk her teeth into Andrew's cock and bit down until her mouth filled with his blood. Though it didn't completely detach Andrew's penis, it did cause him to immediately recoil. He screamed and punched her in the jaw before backing away. Andrew had hurt many women in the past year, and now he was getting his turn to suffer.

"You fucking bitch!" he screamed at her in between his groans. While hunching over he decided now was the time that he would end this once and for all. With his bloody hand he reached down to his pants to pull his gun, not noticing Faith now on her feet and ready to fight back. Faith kicked him in his bloody crotch like she had wanted to do with so many men before. Her toes made direct contact with his balls and sent a wave of shock to Andrew's brain while he was already trying to nurse his mutilated penis. The blows to his self-esteem and his body caused him to drop the gun, giving Faith the miraculous opportunity to take control.

She made a dash for it while Andrew had the same idea. Their hands met on the pistol, both of them fighting with visceral rage.

"Fucking cunt!" Andrew yelled, his adrenaline spiking.
The blood on his hands gave Faith the advantage and soon she was able to strip the gun from Andrew's grip. Now holding the weapon, she didn't think twice about her next move. Without hesitation she quickly aimed the gun at Andrew and pulled the trigger. The bullet hit him in the belly and forced him to hunch over again. The look in his eyes were filled with hatred. He used his last bit of strength to step toward Faith, but she swiftly responded to his resiliency by pulling the trigger two more times and sending the last two bullets into his chest. She pulled the trigger one last time but

only heard the click. Having no more bullets at her disposal she lowered the gun to her side and watched as Andrew fell to the ground.

She was sure that witnesses or the police would be on the scene any minute, so she would need to get away soon. For the moment, however, she found solace in watching Andrew bleed to death on the grass.

26

He was finally out of her life and Faith was once again without anywhere to go. She re-checked the gun to ensure that it was truly out of rounds and then laid it on the ground near Andrew's body. She figured the police would be interested in finding the piece of evidence that would link him to all his other crimes. Faith hoped so anyway. She certainly didn't want any of this coming back to her.

Faith couldn't go back to Richmond, or back to the coast. Cops across the state were looking for the license plates that matched the Camry, so she knew she would have to ditch it soon. Although for now, there was enough money to last until she figured out her next stop.

Driving westward again and approaching the city, Faith reflected on her life; her turbulent upbringing, the boys in school, the lap dances, the drugs, the prostitution. All of it was building up to the lesson she learned that night. Faith had spent too long waiting for someone to swoop in. And now she was finally saving herself.

The sun was rising when she merged onto I-95, driving north with the windows down to let the cool breeze into the car. She wasn't at peace yet, but there was a feeling present that she'd never experienced before – hope.

Faith swore that she would make it to New York City. It was going to take some work for her to fulfill her dreams, but she was ready to take the risks and let her aspirations take charge. Even if her life wasn't the ideal fairy tale that she expected as a young girl, she was satisfied with now being behind the wheel and with the confidence to take care of herself. As she made her way to the Big Apple, Faith felt joy in knowing that she was at last on a path to heal.

Acknowledgements

I'd like to take this moment to thank my beautiful wife for always supporting my creative ventures, no matter how weird, time-consuming, or scatterbrained they might be.

Thank you to authors, Aron Beauregard, Daniel Volpe, Carver Pike, and Rowland Bercy Jr for creating the Written in Red podcast. The episodes were exactly what I needed to kickstart my writing journey and finally publish.

Most importantly, thank you to everyone who picked up this book and made it to the end. It sincerely means the world to me, and I hope you enjoyed the read.

Made in the USA
Middletown, DE
17 March 2025